Room 9-18

Tr3.6.6

© TAKD Entertainment 2016

ISBN: 978-1-365-43518-8

(Book cover by © Gorilla Marketing)

Tr3.6.6

This book includes <u>major</u> contributions from "the real Mya" (Lady LP).
I could not have completed this story without you. This is as much your
story as it is mine. They can keep us apart, but they can never take our
dreams from us.

Love,
Tr3.6.6

—

On the flip side, we changed a lot of stuff in here, which makes this
book fictional. So, for all the critics out there, get over it.

Chapter 1

"Oh!"

That last one was spot on. Mya couldn't help herself. Every fiber of her being was enjoying the moment. Her back stiffened. Her shoulders were thrown back. Her breast bounced in place from the sudden movement. She could feel her stomach cringe with excitement. Her curly hair seemed to straighten almost noticeably. As her body began to relax for a moment, she looked down to view the cause of this transfer of energy. The dim light from the window allowed her to stare into the pair of eyes between her knees. The rest of Don was either beneath her or behind her as she straddled his face like a rider on a robust bull.

She must have moved off target, because his hands were guiding her forward. His right hand cupped the small of her back. He had managed to break free of her grip around his left wrist, which she used to cause Don's hand to fondle her right breast. When she moved, he used his left hand to pull her forward by her slightly wide hips. She eased forward. He delivered a long deliberate stroke with his tongue. She gasped sharply and tried to pull back, but his hold was firmer this time. She looked down again. They never spoke during their sexual encounters, but his eyes delivered a message.

Don't run.

Her eyes delivered one back as her face expressed a warning signal.

I'm about to cum.

He stared back undeterred and sent another message right back.

I know.

She broke the eye contact, relaxed her hips, closed her eyes, and threw her head back. He increased the number of strokes with his tongue, making them more gentle and shorter.

Shit! Mya thought. *I can't take too much more of this without giving in.*

She slowly eased open her legs and leaned back a little. He stopped her from leaning. He swept his tongue from left to right.

She squealed.

Her thighs froze in place to invite more. He did it again in reverse. She shifted left. He placed his hands on top of her thighs to lock her in the position she was in. The rapid-fire flicker of his tongue caused a succession of pulsing surges that flowed through her spine, which caused her to claw at his fingers, and seek something to grab a hold of. She started to quake. He nipped her clit with his lips. She lunged forward; stopping her complete collapse with her palms on the bed. From this angle, she could see the inside of her thighs. They seemed to glow like honey when illuminated by the moonlight. Before her eyes could catch his gaze, he began massaging her button with his tongue, which felt more intense to her in this new position. Her peak was certain and only seconds away.

Three.

She crumpled the sheets just above his head. He felt the tension on the sheets. That was his cue.

Two.

He flattened his tongue to cover more area, but kept the pace the same. Mya began to pant.

One.

Mya fought herself to stay put. She thought about telling Don how disappointed she was that he was late to this rendezvous. At the moment, though, all she could picture was waterfalls.

Zero.

Mya muffled her own scream with her left hand, but her right arm folded under her weight, causing her to double over on top of Don. Don felt a warm liquid rush into his mouth and nose and ooze down the sides of his face before forming pools in his ears.

Moments later, Mya noticed that although his efforts had produced the desired results, Don hadn't stopped. She sat up and looked into his eyes to inquire. Don raised his eyebrows.

What?

She smiled. His eyes told it all. This was only the beginning. He intended to stay a while.

One down...nine to go.

Chapter 2

Thursday, December 24, 2015

Mya awoke the next day in her own bed, not in a hotel room, but she did have a bed guest. It was Don…sort of. Don's junior to be exact. Well, that's what they called him. For a six-year-old sprite, he took up an amazing amount of space. With one arm stretched toward his mother's face and the other folded across his chest, he looked as if he was doing a Michael Jackson impression in his sleep. The thought brought a slight smile to her face, which quickly faded. She realized that her right hand was in her panties and that the moisture on her fingers indicated she had been pleasuring herself in her sleep. Again.

That's twice this week, Mya thought.

She had dreamed up the entire encounter between her and the senior Don. She hadn't dreamed about him in months before that. But now that her meeting with him was just hours away, she had imagined a hopeful scenario in her subconscious. She wanted to believe that's where it would stay.

Physically, she was ready to relieve the sexual tension in her body. However, mentally, she was not ready for the emotional wreck she was going to end up being after she let go of her inhibitions to give in to her urges. The aftermath would be hurricane Katrina. Naturally disastrous. A lot of tears. Walls crashing. Waves of emotions. The thought alone made Mya shudder. At the very least, though, Mya wanted to see him.

It had been nearly five years since she had been able to touch him. And although a lot had happened since then, Mya could never forget the day that she laid eyes on Don for the first time.

Chapter 3

Tuesday, September 18, 2007

Mya overslept. And what's worse, her route from her childhood home to Parkland Hospital was plagued with new construction zones, heavy traffic, and reckless drivers. There was nothing she could do, yet, she dreaded being late for the first day of clinicals. Her professor, Dr. Susan Shields, all but threatened certain removal if any of the students in the program embarrassed the university by being unprofessional. Dr. Seuss, as Sue Shields was referred to amongst her students only, wasn't one to entertain any excuses for perfection. In fact, her favorite word when things were reported favorably was 'perfect'! All of her students unwittingly added the word to their workplace diction. Unfortunately for Mya, picking up an annoying phrase out of habit wasn't the only thing she had to worry about. Punctuality was part of professionalism.

Great. Just great, Mya thought.

Although Parkland Hospital was affiliated with the University of Texas Southwestern Medical Center, Southern Methodist University students were pretty much a shoo-in because the nurse practitioner there was Dr. Seuss' older sister. None of the current class of students had ever met her before clinicals, so they assumed she would be old-looking and blonde with a lot of greys throughout her hair like Dr. Seuss. All they had heard was she could be very uncouth.

Once she finally arrived, Mya parked in the east parking lot, entered the building, and took the nearest elevator to the third floor only to realize that she had to cross over to the west wing to get to the fourth floor, where the pediatric ward was located. By the time she arrived she was—

"Thirty-two minutes late," said the squatty brown-haired woman carrying a clipboard. "You must be Ms. Brown."

"Yes, uh, how do you know that?" Mya asked.

"You're the only one wearing an S-M-U badge that hasn't checked in yet. Let me guess, traffic got you too?" the brunette offered.

"Yes! Yes, I'm glad you understand. I promise not to make a habit out of this, but traffic was terrible. Could we keep this between us? I heard the N-P can be a real bitch like her sister when she wants to," Mya pleaded.

The brunette removed the clipboard cradled in her left arm to reveal the badge attached to her lapel.

Cathy Shields — Nurse Practitioner.

Mya nearly died from embarrassment.

"You're lucky. This new hair color has done wonders for my ego. Everyone thinks I look like a student again," Cathy Shields reported.

I wouldn't say all that, Mya thought.

"I—I didn't mean—"

"Of course you didn't mean to tell me what the other students told you. I'm sure my sister had something to do with that as well," Cathy prodded.

Mya didn't say a word, but she didn't have to.

"Oh, thank you for your honesty, Ms. Brown," Cathy said.

"But I didn't say anything," Mya replied.

"Sure you did. Your skin is fair enough for you to turn the same color of a stop sign. You know, I just decided that I like you," Cathy declared.

"You do?"

"Sure I do. You're honest, ignorant, and pretty all at the same time. You are going to be my personal assistant. Now, tell me. Do you have money for lunch?"

"Yes."

"Good. Now go get me some!" Cathy did an about-face and stormed towards the other students near the nurses' station.

"What do you have a taste for?" Mya called after her.

"Surprise me!" Cathy yelled back.

As Mya entered the elevator, she looked back to see her one sure ally in the program, Lisa, shrugging and mouthing, 'Are you okay?' Mya nodded and disappeared behind the closing doors. Once shielded from the view of others, Mya let out a big sigh and a single tear.

It's gotta get better from here.

Chapter 4

Adonis Lane had only one thing on his mind: five-month-old baby Emilia. It had literally taken hours of convincing from his mother for him to go to the cafeteria for a short break while she kept watch at the baby's side.

Fifteen minutes, no less…Promise.

It had only been three minutes when Adonis began to worry that he had been away too long. There was nothing he could do except wait and hope things would get better. The diagnosis was pneumonia. Adonis couldn't understand how a baby could contract pneumonia in the summer. Well, it was nearly fall, but the temperature hadn't dipped below seventy-five since May. He felt it had to be his fault somehow. Maybe the temperature in the house was too cold. Or the ceiling fan was left on in Emilia's room.

Can that cause her to be sick?

He played multiple scenarios through his head while forcing himself to down a cup of cheap Columbian coffee.

Yuck.

He wasn't a coffee drinker by any means. He just knew that he couldn't stay awake without some form of caffeine. The vending machines were depleted of everything except Coke. He refused to drink that for reasons he didn't care to disclose. It was a mental thing now. He had already been awake for twenty-nine hours straight. He'd wait another two weeks for Emilia to get well if he had to.

Adonis checked the time on his phone to see if it was time for him to go back. By then, only eight minutes had gone by. Staying away for fifteen minutes was the hardest promise he ever had to keep. All he wanted to do was be there when little Emilia opened her eyes. She had been resting for quite a while, but the doctor assured Don that was normal in these circumstances.

Adonis was the only one in the room besides the kitchen staff until a nurse walked in. From her hurried movements, Adonis first thought she might be looking for him until she made a beeline for the counter. He relaxed a little. He realized that he had never seen her before. Not that the hospital was his favorite place to pick up women. Besides, he was married. However, as beautiful as she was, he would definitely know if he'd seen her before.

Maybe she...

Adonis shook the thought out of his head. He stood and decided that, if he walked slowly, the next five minutes would go by before he made it back to Emilia's bedside. Factor in wait time for the elevator and you have fifteen minutes exactly.

He pressed the up button for the elevator.

Come on, come on.

He preferred to ride the elevator alone. A few more minutes of peace without some little kid pressing every button causing the elevator to stop on every floor. Was that too much to ask?

The elevator chime sounded and the door opened. It had appeared that he got his wish. He entered the elevator and pressed the button for the fourth floor.

"I made it," said the woman behind a mountain of cellophane. It was the nurse from the cafeteria. "Could you press four for me, please?"

"That's where I'm headed," Adonis replied.

"Perfect," said the nurse. Her face was barely visible from the side.

"Can I help you with some of that? You look like you have enough food for a small army," Adonis commented.

"No, just one general. But, I could use some help," she said.
Adonis took all but one tray. He figured he could drop off the food at the nurses' station on the way to Emilia's room.

"You're a student," Adonis said. "That's why I haven't seen you around before."

Mya looked down at her badge, then up at Adonis and smiled sheepishly.

"Yeah, I am."

The elevator door opened.

"Lead the way, general," Adonis said.

Mya smiled. The nickname from a complete stranger flattered her more than she realized. She was nearly high stepping by the time she made it to the nurses' station. Brenda, an overweight, tenured nurse seated at the computer, gave Mya a bug-eyed look. Mya assumed that Brenda was shocked she had managed to get such a handsome escort in less than half an hour of being on the job. As Adonis set the food on the counter of the nurses' station, a Latin woman wearing black scrubs ran up to him and embraced him from the side.

"There you are baby! I look for you," she said.

"I just got back from taking a break," Adonis replied.

"It look like you buy food for all the nurse. You no have to do that. They take good care of Millie," the Latin woman said.

"I know, Val. But, as much as I would like to take credit for treating your lovely co-workers to lunch, I have to admit it wasn't me. However, I did help carry it on my way back," Adonis explained.

"Aw. You always help people. Come now. Let's go check on Millie," Val said as she extended her hand to him. He grabbed her hand and the two interlocked their fingers and walked side by side to Emilia's room.

"Girl, are you crazy?" Brenda asked Mya.

A startled Mya stopped gawking immediately and turned her attention to Brenda.

"Who was that?" Mya asked.

"Valencia Lane. She works pharmacy. And *he* is her husband," Brenda explained.

"Does he work here?" Mya asked.

"No. His little girl is on this floor. Val is the little girl's mother. And you are just a little too nosey for your own good."

"*Excuse me.* I just know a good-looking man when I see one. Besides, he wasn't wearing a ring."

"Oh he's just hurt, that's all. He'll forgive Val eventually. And he does wear his ring. Not on his finger, but on the necklace her wears."

"What's there to forgive?"

"There you go being nosey again."

"I see."

"What's with all the food? You eating for two today?"

"No. Miss Shields sent me for lunch and I had no clue what she would like. I asked the cafeteria lady what Ms. Shields usually ordered and she told me these four things, so I just bought them all. Just in case," Mya explained.

"You're either really smart, really dumb, or got a rich father," Brenda said.

Brenda's analysis of Mya wasn't too far off. Mya lived a privileged life with very few bumps in the road. Her father was the well-known Senator Jamerson E. Brown, who spent recent years teaching legislation at the University of Texas in Austin. Mya's mother, Virginia Brown, was a retired ballet instructor who taught at Juilliard. The Browns were determined to make sure their children had every opportunity allotted to them, but instilled in them moral values, humility, love, and kindness. At the moment, Mya was trying to improve on her butchered first impression.

"Oh crap!" Mya said.

"Don't stress. Just send her the tuna. Today is tuna Tuesday for her," Brenda said.

"No not that," Mya said.

"Then what, child?" Brenda asked.

"Nothing. I just realized something," Mya said as her embarrassed grin turned into full-blown laughter. Mya told Adonis the food was for one general.

He thinks I'm the general!

Chapter 5

Near the end of her shift, Mya peeked into room 402 hoping not to be noticed. She just wanted a glimpse of Adonis and the rumored-to-be most beautiful baby in the world that all the nurses raved about. But a guy like Adonis noticed everything.

"Do you need something?" Adonis asked.

Mya awkwardly froze in place then entered the room, stepping just inside of the door.

"Um, I was just stopping by to see if Mrs. Lane was in here," Mya lied.

Adonis offered her no reaction then turned his attention back to Emilia. He gently stroked the baby girl's forearm with his index finger. Watching him was sweet and heartbreaking at the same time. He doted over his baby girl more than any man Mya had ever met. Of course, she knew her own father loved her. But, this seemed to be a different level of love that she hadn't witnessed from a father. The situation wasn't as dire as Mya first thought. She figured Emilia had a tumor the way everyone jumped up to check on her.

Is that the reason why he is so concerned? Has anybody told him?

Mya took two small steps forward.

"If it's any solace, walking pneumonia is not usually dangerous," Mya said softly.

"Not usually?" Adonis asked sharply.

Mya panicked. His answer indicated that he focused on the words that implied that there could be a problem.

He sensed she regretted her words.

"Relax," Adonis said. I know all about walking pneumonia."

"Oh. So you went to school of some sort," Mya said. It didn't come out as smooth as she would have liked.

"You can say that," Adonis said.

"Where did you study at?"

"University of Google, courtesy of Sprint. They have great online courses."

"Oh. I thought you meant—"

"I know. That was mean, but you left the door open and I couldn't help it. Besides," Adonis paused as he chuckled a bit. "I needed the laugh."

Mya relaxed a little and offered a smile.

Am I smiling too hard?

"You're welcome?" Mya asked.

"Yeah. Thank you. I'll be sure to tell Cathy about your excellent bedside manner," Adonis said.

"That would be greatly appreciated," Mya said.

"No problem," Adonis said.

Mya turned to look at the doorway then back at Adonis. She fixed her mouth to say something but thought better of it. Instead, she said,

"When you do talk to Cathy, my name is Mya Brown."

"I know."

"The badge. Right. I'll leave you now."

She left.

As soon as she stepped out of the room, she bumped into Jarin, a five-ten, third-year linebacker that Mya had dated off and on since they were both college freshmen. At that moment, they were off.

"What are you doing here?" Mya asked.

"Lisa told me that you would be up here so I wanted to surprise you with this," Jarin said as he presented a single rose to her that he was concealing behind his back.

"What is that for?" Mya asked.

"It represents us. You know, a new beginning," Jarin said.

"Really, well it's fitting that you picked a flower," Mya said.

"Yeah, I know."

"It really fits our relationship."

"That's why I got it."

"Because just like our relationship, this flower will be dead in a few days." Mya pushed him away from her and walked away briskly towards the nurses' station.

"Mya, don't be like that," Jarin said.

She ignored him and updated a few charts.

"You gonna be like that? Bet," Jarin said and then left.

———

While he was walking to his truck in the parking lot, a sunburst yellow Chevy Aveo pulled up next to him.

"There you are," he said.

"Who does that belong to?" the woman driver asked.

"Oh *this*?" Jarin said referring to the rose. "This is for you."

"Then give it to me," she said.

"My truck has more room."

"No, no, no. No parking lot sex this time. Meet me at the apartment."

"Where is he?"

"Not home."

"On my way."

"Do not make me wait for you."

Chapter 6

Friday, December 7, 2007

He did not intend to meet up with her that night. Honestly, he didn't know she was there. All he knew was Rich said there was an event at the Green Elephant on Dyer Street and that everybody would be there. He really wasn't supposed to be there. He hadn't been a student in over a year. His class graduated in the spring without him. He was only a resident in the area because his wife insisted on living near campus. But, anyone that knew him, mainly the current class of seniors, knew that Don (as they called him) was the man. If Don was at your party, the ladies would be thoroughly entertained and he (and by extension those associated with him) was going to get laid. Therefore, he pretty much had a V.I.P pass to any event hosted by SMU students.

Don never showed up at any party on time. The first hours were usually a memory before he made an appearance. A good indication that he had arrived was a crowded dance floor, a change in music from okay to great, and people taking their shirts off. Ladies included.

Don wore his favorite red Old Navy jacket that his ex-fiancée bought for him for his twenty-first birthday. Underneath, he wore a white beater. He also wore blue South Pole jeans and a black fitted Atlanta Braves baseball cap that he used to hide his eyes as he surveyed the crowd. An instinctive habit that he picked up in the projects of South Dallas taught him to scope out possible enemies before having fun. The coast was clear that night. He then looked for the quickest way to make the night memorable.

Chapter 7

Don and Rich had known each other since 2003 when they were both entering as freshmen. They met at freshmen orientation camp held at a ranch in Arlington. The freshmen class of that year was bigger than normal due to the combined number of dropouts from the three previous classes. Yet, despite the absence of the in-season collegiate athletes, there wasn't enough room to house all of the freshmen in the infamous barracks. As a result, Don, whose legal name was Adonis Lane, was one of the fortunate few that were selected to house with the orientation staff in the ranch hotel. Richard Williams wasn't.

The hotel was conveniently located near the pool and the outdoor basketball court. So, after Don proved his athletic dominance on the court, he would take a dip in the shallow end of the pool, making sure that the ladies in the vicinity had a great view of his well-defined abs. Rich noticed the droves of incoming freshmen women Don attracted. It didn't bother him until the one he had his eye on told Rich that Don invited her and two other women to hang out at his room instead of sleeping in the insect-infested barracks. Sleeping bags, hotel room, and women in scant clothing. Can't beat that without adding alcohol to the equation. That was when the envy started to set in.

Rich was taller than Don — six-two versus five-eight. However, if they were competing, the attributes favored Don by a landslide. Yeah, Don grew up underprivileged, but he was much smarter than he presented himself to be. He had an air of confidence that bordered exorbitant arrogance, yet a mysterious smile that begged innocence and sexiness simultaneously. It helped that he was handsome with deep dark brown eyes that you would swear could look through you. He wasn't lanky like Rich but a toned version of skinny. Fit. Rich was on the track team, but he was oddly shaped; a little pudgy around the waist. Almost a one to one chest to waistline ratio. He wore glasses, but if you put the same glasses on Don, he would be adorable. They just didn't work for Rich. He had a crooked smile, acne, and a timid personality when it came to approaching women. In other words, Rich was no Don. He just wasn't.

Rich began badmouthing Don because he was jealous of all the attention Don was getting. Don didn't retaliate with words. He outwitted Rich by inviting him to join the slumber party. Don figured that since the ladies outnumbered guys by one, there would be someone to keep the last woman occupied if she happened to be a cock blocker. Don only invited three women to spend the night and one quick friend he made at the pool— Jeremy — a former body builder. Besides Rich would likely be humiliated by the female company. Don figured that even if one of the women put their pussy in Rich's hand, he wouldn't know what to do with it. His words. Rich readily accepted Don's invitation and immediately regretted talking crap about him. He became Don's wingman once they returned to campus and kept Don informed about every event on and off campus.

Chapter 8

Don wasn't just having a bad night; he was having a bad year. Well, nearly two years. His girlfriend and his son were killed in the spring of 2006. His grandfather was murdered in June of that same year. Valencia discovers she was pregnant in July and threatened to abort the child unless he promised to marry her. Soon after the baby was born, he married her, but found out that she was sleeping around within months of getting married. He had no concrete evidence yet, but the rumors were flying. On the night of the party, Don felt as if the walls of his own home were caving in on him. There was nothing he wanted to do more than create a memory that would temporarily replace his current thoughts.

When night fell and his seven-month-old baby girl was sleeping, he crawled out of bed (where his wife was asleep) and got dressed. Before leaving, he checked one last time to make sure his daughter was okay, kissed her on the cheek and whispered,

"I promise I'll be back before you wake up."

Don decided not to drive that night, but he didn't need a ride either. His second-floor apartment in Amesbury Parc was less than a mile from the SMU campus. He walked as if he was aimlessly traveling without a destination in mind. His course was already set. Fate kept his feet in motion.

Chapter 9

Friday, December 7, 2007

Lisa convinced Mya to accompany her for a night out. The school term was nearly over and their stint at Parkland was approaching three months. It was every bit as stressful as advertised. Mya at times felt as if she was struggling to keep up with her demanding schedule. She hadn't attempted to rekindle her relationship with Jarin, but couldn't help but think of him that night. It was his birthday. Jarin, though, hadn't attempted to contact Mya at all.

Lisa and Mya first stopped by the Barley House to survey the crowd and throw back a couple of shots. The bar was relatively quiet and hosted a subdued crowd with only a handful of rowdy patrons.

Boring.

The pair then decided to go to the Green Elephant on Dreyer. They were early so they decided to grab a quick bite to eat at Kuby's Sausage House on Snider Plaza before returning. By the time they returned to the bar, a sizable crowd had formed. Lisa maneuvered her way through the crowd while Mya followed by holding onto Lisa's trailing hand. They finally settled by a wall near the dance floor. Mya received a text from Jarin.

"Party on me in Melrose" Jarin texted.

"Warwick Melrose in not the same as THE Melrose." Mya replied.

"Close enough. You coming?" Jarin asked via text.

"And why would my company matter to you tonight?" Mya shot back.

"Because. It's you. No one can replace you." Jarin answered.

"Says the man who hasn't texted or called me since this summer. You forgot my birthday." Mya replied.

"I didn't forget. I thought you were mad at me."

"I was! You forgot my birthday!"

"You forgot mine."

"Yours isn't over yet. And no I didn't."

"Well let's have a joint party. Just me and you."

"I'll think about it."

"Don't think. Just come."

"Now?"

"Yes."

"You have company and I'm out with Lisa."

"By the time you get here, everyone will be gone."

"What made you get a hotel?"

"Wishful thinking."

Mya laughed aloud before texting back. "Keep wishing."

"So, are you coming?" Jarin asked.

"We'll see. I'll text you later."

"You know where it is right?"

"Yeah Oak Lawn Ave. Ttyl."

Chapter 10

"I've seen her before," Don said referring to the woman with light skin trailing the shorter white woman.

"Which one?" Rich Asked.

"The one wearing the wool sweater, tight blue jeans, and the running shoes," Don said.

"That's Mya Brown," Rich said.

"Mya Brown…yeah, the nursing chick."

"Last I heard she was messing with Watts."

"The lame ranger?"

"Ha, ha. You foul for that. He got skill. That's why they call him 'the game changer'," Rich explained.

"He'll never go pro. What's the status?" Don asked.

"Well some speculate that if he has another good year, he'll be a third round—"

"Not his status! Hers."

"Oh, my bad. I don't know. She's been a ghost. I can ask Lisa."

"Who's that?"

"The chick with her."

"How tall is that white chick?" Don asked.

"About five foot even. Why?" Rich asked.

"That makes Mya about five-two."

"What else can you tell from over here?"

"That form-fitting sweater tells me she has a secret body she doesn't want everybody to know about. I list her at thirty-six, twenty-four, thirty-six."

"Man, hell nah!"

"What you wanna bet?"

"How will you get the answer?"

"Trust me, it won't take long." Don said.

"Sounds like another wager," Rich taunted.

"I bet you tonight's tab that I'll have her by the end of the night."

"I don't know. You're not the same ole Don. Besides, she's probably texting her man right now. What kind of single woman comes to a bar, doesn't drink, dance, nothing?" Rich asked.

"A designated driver and a woman that hasn't met me. Let's go. You got the white girl," Don said before making his way to Mya.

From the direction they approached the two women, Don realized that they would encounter Lisa from behind. Mya was leaning against the wall on her left shoulder. Lisa was facing Mya and the two were discussing heading over to Jarin's hotel party. Don made a last second decision to fall behind, allow Rich to play the familiar face game with Lisa, and allow himself to be introduced. Mya looked up from her phone momentarily to signal to Lisa about the two approaching them. Lisa turned to see Rich.

"Hey!" Lisa called out elatedly then threw her arms around Rich. On cue, Rich picked her up, did a half turn, and set her down in front of Don.

"What are you doing here? I thought you were in grad school?" Lisa asked.

"I'm on break. Decided to come and see who I would run into. I brought my boy with me," Rich said as he gestured to Don. Lisa turned to look.

"I'm Lisa," she said reaching to hug Don.

"Don," he said in her ear as he hugged her.

Just then, Montell Jordan's "This Is How We Do It" sounded through the speakers. Don rocked Lisa to the beat, released his hold, and invited her to dance. She went along with it right where they stood.

"Get her, Don! Break her off!" Rich called out in a playful manner. Lisa turned around and backed into Don. Then, she invited Rich to join them by dancing in front of her. Mya looked on and sent one last text as Lisa enjoyed being sandwiched between the two men.

Suddenly, Don broke away and briefly said something in a waiter's ear before making his way over to Mya. He approached half walking, half dancing, but in rhythm and on beat. Mya wore a half smile, curious as to whom the mystery man was. She couldn't see his eyes because the brim of his hat was so low. He grabbed her hands and gently pulled her toward him. She followed hesitantly. He placed her hands on his shoulders then placed his own hands on her hips. She decided that one dance wouldn't hurt. That's when he looked up and stared into her eyes. She laughed and fell into him while burying her face into his shoulder.

"So, you *do* remember me," Don said.

"Not by name," Mya said.

"Is that so, Mya Brown?" Don asked.

Tr3.6.6

She looked up as if she was stunned that he remembered her name. She smiled at him.

"How's Cathy treating you?" Don asked.

"Not bad. Not good," Mya said.

"Dance with me for one more song and I'll see about convincing her to take something off of you."

Mya laughed. "Deal."

Chapter 11

By the time the next song ended, a waiter arrived with a round of strawberry rum and Coke for Rich, Lisa, and Mya. Don just took a double shot of strawberry rum. No Coke. He then requested another round for everyone except himself. Five songs later Don and Mya hadn't stopped dancing. Mya progressively became more touchy feely. Rich and Lisa were content with just talking and catching up with each other. They also watched Don and Mya go at it.

The deejay finally cut in to introduce some sort of contest on stage, which meant there was a break before the next song. Don took that moment to excuse himself and step outside to cool off. Rich followed, carrying his drink with him.

"Damn bro! Is she gonna let you breathe?" Rich asked.

"Man, this is too easy. I still got it," Don said.

"You don't have to prove nothing to me, married man," Rich said.

"You had to go there, huh?" Don asked.

"My bad. So what's the game plan?" Rich asked.

"To make her remember me," Don said.

"That's all?"

"Well, anything extra would be a plus."

"Like…"

Don took off his jacket, removed his beater and put his jacket back on. He lowered his brim and put the hood to his jacket over his fitted cap.

"Give me a piece of ice from your drink," Don said.

"And what do you plan on doing with this?" Rich asked as he handed it over to Don.

"Nothing," Don said. He then rubbed the ice between his hands and clutched it in his right fist. "Let's go."

They started back. Again, Don fell behind as Rich led the way. Rich made it back to Lisa's side, but Don kept walking as if he was going to pass Mya. She grabbed him by his right arm with both hands.

Gotcha, Mya thought.

Gotcha, Don thought.

Kanye West's "Stronger" began playing.

Mya grabbed Don by the wrist and guided his hands to her hips. Don tossed the remaining piece of ice behind Mya. Mya removed Don's hood and lifted Don's brim to see his eyes. She then allowed her hand to slip from his neck to his chest and then his stomach. Don managed to slip his right hand under Mya's sweater. He brushed his cool hand against her left side then traced the waistband of her jeans, just below her naval. She caught his hand, smiled, and then placed it on her stomach. He moved it to her back pocket and pulled her closer. She laughed. She took off his cap and placed it on her own head, brim backwards.

Hours went by. Last call was announced. Mya and Don remained pressed up against one another. Rich and Lisa had run out of things to talk about except how Mya and Don looked together. The party was sure to end for the night soon. The current song was half over and was likely the last song of the night. That's when it happened. Mya went for it. She kissed him. Don went along with it. Of course, he was married, but he wasn't thinking about that right then. What initially started out as a challenge turned into something more. But, what?

Another song began. Neither Don nor Mya could recall the name of the song. It's not clear that either of them actually heard it. All it meant was that they had more time to enjoy the moment.

The lights flashed on and off. Patrons started filing out. Rich and Lisa laughed awkwardly about their friends, turned away, and headed to the exit. Mya's phone vibrated. Don thought nothing of it because she had ignored since they began dancing. Suddenly, though, Mya broke away. She ran to catch up with Lisa and the two quickly made their way out the door.

Rich waited for Don to catch up.

"What was that about?" Rich asked.

"Which part?" Don asked back. "The dancing, the kissing, or the sudden break for it?"

"In either case, it seems you jinxed yourself by paying for the drinks."

Chapter 12

"Oh my gosh, Lisa!" Mya exclaimed. "Do you realize who that was?"

"No, I just met him," Lisa replied.

"You know Valencia from the hospital?" Mya asked.

"The pharmacy slut?" Lisa clarified.

"Yes her." Mya said.

"What about her? Is she boning him?"

"I don't know about all that, but she is his wife."

"Oh my gosh! Good for you!"

"No, not good for me!"

"What do you mean? It's about time she gets hers."

"Get hers?"

"Yeah. You know, payback!"

"What are you saying?" Mya asked.

Lisa paused to look at Mya. Lisa realized that Mya assumed she was insinuating something.

"I'm just saying that…payback is a bitch. Even for a bitch," Lisa said calmly.

Mya turned to look back at the bar, then back at Lisa. She smiled.

"You're right. How are you getting home?" Mya asked.

"I live on campus. I'll just walk with the mass of people heading back. I'll be safe with them. How are you getting home?" Lisa asked.

"I'm not going directly home, but a cab will get me where I'm going. I'll text you to let you know I made it safely."

"You should—" Lisa started but stopped when she thought about it. "Have fun, Mya."

"I will. I need to *unwind* a bit," Mya said.

A short cab drive later, Mya arrived at Warwick Melrose. She was somewhat out of it. Not intoxicated, but giddy and playing with her lips. She was thinking about Don. Jarin answered the door with a grin on his face. He was wearing only his boxers. Mya shook her head still smiling.

"I'll take that as a compliment," Jarin said.

"You're not what I want, but you're the best that I can do on such short notice," Mya replied.

"I'll take that, too. Get in here."

Tr3.6.6

Chapter 13

Tuesday, December 11, 2007

Mya was still livid by the time she arrived at Parkland for clinicals.

She hadn't found them right away, but after Jarin was satisfied, she stretched her arms upward and slipped her hands under one of the pillows. That's when she found them. Black, lace panties — size small.

Mya hopped out of bed immediately and started getting dressed. Jarin returned from the bathroom only to see Mya hurriedly zipping up her jeans. Mya threw the unfamiliar panties at him. Of course, he offered the classic response.

"Those aren't yours?"

Mya didn't dignify his question with an answer. She slipped on her sweater and walked out the door.

There was a cab dropping off a rider as she exited the building. She hopped in and paid the driver in advance before she could say he was off duty or headed to pick up another customer. After she gave the driver directions, she called Lisa. Mya had to tell her what a pig Jarin was. However, as soon as Lisa picked up, an eerie feeling came over her.

"Hello? Mya? You there?" Lisa asked.

"How long?" Mya asked.

"How long, what?" Lisa sounded confused.

"How long have you known, Lisa?" Mya fired back.

"I don't—"

"Lisa! Just tell me. How long have you known?"

Lisa sighed heavily before answering. "I didn't know for sure until last week. I overheard her—"

"You know who it is?" Mya sounded pained.

The elevator opened. Mya shook the thought of the weekend's events out of her mind. At some point of the shift, she was sure to see Lisa.

Mya could hear Brenda laughing before she could even see the nurses' station. What Mya didn't know was the cause of her laughter. There was a small crowd of people including Cathy gathered around with their cell phones snapping pictures, recording video and chanting.

"Go Millie, go Millie…" they cheered.

He's here.

Mya thought about avoiding the desk temporarily, but she had to check-in with Brenda. Moreover, for the first time, she could show Cathy that she was not only punctual, but early. With the exception of day one, Mya was early every day. Cathy never seemed to notice because she was never present when Mya arrived. All she cared about is that Mya was there. And on time.

But, what about Don? She hadn't spoken to him since their encounter at the bar. She didn't explain her actions that night. She wasn't sure if she wanted to, considering how things turned out.

Maybe he won't say anything about it.

Mya approached to get a better view of baby Millie. She partially concealed her huge grin behind a blue pacifier with "Daddy's girl" printed on it. She focused on her Daddy's face as she half squatted in place while grasping firmly on his fingers with both hands. Despite the drool pouring down her chin, Millie was the most adorable baby Mya had ever seen. Emilia had gained quite a bit of weight since Mya had last seen her. It was nice to see her healthy and full of energy. That's what she joined the nursing program for. Moments like that.

"Okay, Boobie, show's over," Don said as he lifted Millie and settled her in his right arm.

"Aw, so soon?" Cathy asked.

"We have to make the not-so-short drive to Houston to see Nana today," Don said.

"How is your mother doing?" Cathy asked.

"She's recovering. I'm actually bringing her home today. Instead of driving my gas guzzler, I'm trading cars with Val," Don said.

"You can leave Millie with me," Cathy suggested.

"No way. Besides, you have your own babies to look after," Don said while nodding towards Mya.

Cathy turned to Mya. "There's my early bird. Keep up the good work, Mya."

Mya was taken aback. Cathy's endearing words were completely random. Mya looked at Don then back at Cathy.

"Thanks," Mya said.

Cathy turned her attention back to Don. "Well, at least allow me to carry the diaper bag down to the car so I can see my babies off."

Brenda cut in, "Cathy, you have an important phone call on line two."

"Oh poo," Cathy said.

"I see you've been practicing your nice words around Millie," Don teased.

"With a baby that beautiful, you don't have to try. It just comes naturally. I sure miss you. I wish you would have stayed with the program. You would have made a wonderful nurse," Cathy commented.

"But, then there would be no Millie," Don said.

"I'm sure you would have managed to squeeze her in somehow. Here, allow me to put the blanket over her. It's cold out there," Cathy said.

Don braced Millie against his chest while Cathy draped the blanket over the baby girl.

"Now how are you gonna make sure the blanket doesn't come off her head and carry this diaper bag at the same time?" Cathy asked.

"I'll manage," Don said.

"I can carry it," Mya volunteered before she realized what she said. "I mean…I'm a little early. I can go and come back before it's time to get started."

Cathy didn't think much of it. "Okay, eager beaver. You carry it." Cathy then stood on her toes to kiss Don on the cheek. "Be careful, you hear? Give your mother my best."

The elevator ride was uneventful and awkward. Don didn't try to look in Mya's direction. Mya was afraid to attempt to make eye contact with Don. Fortunately, for both of them, they were only on the fourth floor.

Once outside, Mya decided to break the ice.

"Which car is yours?" she asked.

"We're headed over to that yellow Chevy," Don said.

"The keys are in the diaper bag."

Mya fished them out before they arrived at the car. She unlocked the doors for him and waited as he fastened Emilia in her car seat. She then handed over the diaper bag and keys.

"Thanks," Don said.

"Thank you as well," Mya said. "She's never been that kind to me."

"I was just keeping my end of the deal. Besides, she knows she needs to make the good ones feel as if they belong there," Don explained.

Mya stood close as if to invite Don to kiss her. He didn't.

"I gotta get going. Maybe I'll see you around. That is if you don't have to run off," Don teased.

He opened the driver's door. Mya didn't know what to say. She knew he was teasing, but she didn't have the nerve to shoot back or explain.

"Goodbye, general," Don said as he closed the door. Mya stayed in the parking lot until he drove off. He stopped at the end of the parking lot. Mya imagined that he wanted her to run up to the car and ride off to Houston with him. Just as she took a hopeful step in his direction, he pulled into the traffic.

Valencia and another pharmacy technician were waiting on Mya when she reentered the building. No one said a word. They just exchanged dirty looks.

Mya stepped onto the elevator. When the door shut, she closed her eyes.

I wonder what he thinks about me. Maybe…no way. Now, that is wishful thinking.

Chapter 14

Don had just closed the door to the Chevy leaving Mya in the cold. He fumbled the keys as he tried to figure out why she would spend hours with him exclusively and still rush out as if she had somewhere to be. Maybe Rich was right. What kind of single woman goes to a bar only to be heavily distracted by her phone? Don finally got the key in the ignition and started the car. He made one last passing glance in her direction before backing out of the parking space.

You can't expect a beautiful woman like that to be single, Don thought.

Don stopped at the end of the parking lot. He remembered that he had to remind Val several times to put the updated insurance card in the glove compartment. He wasn't sure that she did. When he opened the glove compartment, old dried up rose pedals and a stem fell onto the floorboard. Don thought nothing of it. But, he wouldn't ignore the note on top of the insurance card. It was handwritten.

It read:

Tr3.6.6

```
    She  knows  now.  I  did  my  part.  It's  now
your  turn  to  dump  him.  Don't  make  me  wait  for
you.
```
                    -Jarin

Don felt his blood boil. But, there were more pertinent issues at hand. Starting with the insurance. The card was the correct one. Now to pick up Mama. Don noticed, when looking in the rearview mirror, that Mya was still standing there in the parking lot.

If only you were single, Mya Brown.

Don drove off.

Chapter 15

Friday, December 14, 2007

Don took the rest of the workweek off to help his mother get settled in. He chose to spend a couple of days in Houston to decide what his next move was going to be, but he didn't plan on being gone longer than a day. The day after he left for Houston, a snowstorm blew in that covered Southern parts of Kansas to northern parts of Texas. That was the excuse he used to stay away. He managed to bring his mother home safely Thursday night.

Valencia had no clue that Don had discovered the letter. In fact, before Don returned the car to her, he put the letter, the stem, and the pedals back into the glove compartment. Now that his mother was settled in, he attempted to enjoy the rest of his time off.

"Daddy's bored, Millie," Don said as he sprawled out in front of his laptop on the queen size bed in Millie's room. Millie was nearly asleep in her crib — afternoon naptime. She wouldn't sleep unless her daddy was in the room, so Don decided to piddle around on Facebook.

I wonder if she's on here.

He searched for Mya Brown. It didn't take long for him to find her. Her profile picture was that of her, Lisa, and another woman Don didn't know. Don thought about sending her a message, but he didn't know what to say, so he used the poke option instead. He then viewed her past profile pictures. A few had other women Don didn't know, some had Lisa, and others had a guy he recognized by face but not by name. He wasn't tagged in the photos either. Lisa made comments about them being a cute couple but didn't mention any names. The date indicated it was posted in the spring.

Could this be who she was texting?

Don was starting to think he was spinning his wheels when he clicked on the home page and noticed that he had a new notification. Mya had poked him back.

Is she on right now?

Don decided to send Mya a message. He couldn't think of anything intelligent to say. He hadn't read her page to find out what her likes and dislikes were, her background, or any of that. It seemed a bit cliché to talk about the weather, but that was all he had.

"Keeping warm?"

That was the entire message he sent. He figured that it wasn't being too inquisitive, yet it was considerate and showed a level of concern. Mya focused on how considerate it was. She responded.

"Yes, I've managed to do so. Thanks for asking. How's the baby girl?"

"She's great. Catching up on her beauty rest at the moment." Don replied.

"Ah. So that's the secret to her beauty! Lol" Mya joked.

"I like to think that my good genes had something to do with it." Don typed.

"Lol. Aw, how humble of you." Mya shot back.

"Yeah, I think so too. Any major plans? It's winter break for you all."

"No. Just stuck at home with my parents."

"Oh. You've already left for home. How far is that?"

"I live in Dallas Lol"

"Ah. Why didn't you just stay on campus?"

"I've never lived on campus."

"Oh. You're one of those…LOL"

"What is one of those?" Mya asked.

"Daddy's girl. He's gotta keep an eye on you. Lol there's nothing wrong with that. Millie will be at home until she is 44." Don explained.

"Lol good luck with that!"

"Yeah I know. But a father can dream, can't I?"

"I'm sure she'll make good decisions as an adult."

Don started to make a comment about hoping Emilia doesn't turn out to be like Valencia, but he erased it. Mya didn't wait for him to respond.

"So the name Don. Is that short for Donnie or something?" Mya asked.

"Adonis." Don said.

"That's quite a name to live up to. Lol" Mya commented.

"Why do you say that? Don asked.

"I'm kinda into the meaning of names."

"Why? Do you plan on having kids sometime soon?"

"Yes, but that's not why."

"So you're pregnant?"

"No! LOL"

"Oh. Just checking."

"Meanings of names just intrigue me."

"So what does my name mean?"

"Lord."

"Oh. Didn't know that. But that's not why I was named Adonis."

"Is it because an Adonis is a very handsome man by definition?"

"Nope, although it fits."

"So humble. Lol" Mya said, again being sarcastic.

"Yeah, I know." Don replied with sarcasm of his own.

"So tell me." Mya said. "Why were you named Adonis?"

"Because my mom said that she was sure I would be everything that A DON IS. Get it?"

"A mafia leader? Lol"

"No, dictionary queen! Lol"

"Then what?"

"A gentleman."

"Oh. Aw, that was sweet of her."

Don wasn't ready for the warmth that came from the compliments and the generosity Mya offered him. He made up some lame excuse about having to leave because Millie was waking up. He lied.

Mya went with it though. He hadn't logged off for ten minutes and she already missed him. Two words were all it took to get Mya feeling an array of emotions.

"Keeping warm?"

Chapter 16

Valencia rushed in the front door of her apartment. She was frantic.

"Don-Don? Millie? Don-Don, where are you?" Valencia called out.

Don jumped up from his relaxed position on the bed in Millie's room. He hurried to the door, opened it quietly, and shut it behind him as quickly and softly as he could. He held up a hand to Valencia as he approached to calm her and alert her that Millie was sleeping.

"What's wrong?" Don said softly.

"It's Mami, it's Mami, it's Mami!" Valencia said.

"Calm down, Val. Calm down. Nothing can be solved in the next few minutes. I need you to explain to me what's wrong with Mami," Don said calmly.

Don guided her by the shoulders to the couch. She sat down and pulled out a used wad of tissue from the pocket of the scrubs she was wearing. She spoke only between sobs.

"Mami... she sick," Valencia said.

"Okay. How sick?" Don asked.

"Carlita said she has the…no memory. You know? The no memory. Now Carlita say…she soon die," Valencia explained.

Don seemed to struggle to understand. Even after being with her for over a year, he found it hard to decipher what she meant at times. Her English was great when she took her time. Don often said her English was worse when she got upset.

"Val, do you mean Alzheimer's disease? Your mother has Alzheimer's?" Don asked.

"Jes," Valencia replied.

"That's a progressive disease, Val. She wouldn't die in a matter of days."

"No, she have…" She continued, but the words were indistinct.

"How long has she had it? Why didn't your sister tell you before today?"

"Porque…she no want me worry, Don-Don. You know, how I get."

"Okay, so what's next? What do you want to do?" Don asked.

"I go to her." Valencia said adamantly.

"That's understood."

"Come with?"

Don hesitated. He was anguished about the situation. He had a passport. He always wanted to go to South America. He felt for Valencia and her family. But, he couldn't forgive Valencia's indiscretions involving at least one other man.

"I can't, Val." Don said.

"Why not?" Valencia asked.

"I just can't. Not now. I'm sorry."

"Please, Don-Don, please! I no go home without you, Don-Don. Please! Por Millie."

"One of us has to work, Val. Besides, your family hates me."

"No hate, Don-Don. They no get it."

"Have you explained to them that I am not who they think I am?"

"I try."

"Yeah, well, now you'll have plenty of time."

Don stood from his position on the couch and walked towards the bedroom.

"Can I take Millie?" Valencia asked.

Don stopped dead in his tracks, turned to Val, and got directly in her face.

"You don't bathe her, feed her, burp her, change her diaper, or even hold her for extended periods of time. You're quick to put her down for a nap when she's in your way like when you want to have sex with me. Unless someone makes a comment about her in public, you don't even mention her. And you expect me to trust you to look out for her overseas?" Don asked.

"She family," Valencia mumbled.

"What does that mean?"

"No harm come to her. I promise."

"Your promise doesn't mean shit to me when it comes to my daughter!"

"I keep my promise to have her, remember?"

"Yeah, because I wouldn't have married you otherwise. She was nothing more than a hostage to you at the time. Leverage for negotiation."

"Without her, I no have you. I know. I'm not eh-stupid."

"At least you know."

Tears streamed down Valencia's face the second he said that.

"I never really had you. Did I?" Valencia asked softly.

Don backed up and turned away from her.

"I married you, didn't I?" Don replied. "Look, I trust Carlita. When you start feeling like you don't want to be bothered, make sure you have Carlita looking after Millie."

"Promise."

Don turned to face Valencia. "When do you leave?"

Val stood and faced Don. "Tonight."

Chapter 17

Saturday December 15, 2007 — 2:47 AM

Several hours after their plane departed, Don was still awake in bed thinking about his baby girl. The longest he had been away from her was just under 13 hours when he worked twelve-hour shifts at his job. He appeared to be stoic as he kissed his wife and daughter goodbye. He even drove to the apartment without looking back once. However, once he climbed into bed, the dams could no longer hold the water and he cried so hard it made him physically ill. He ran to the bathroom and vomited as if he had too much to drink, crawled into bed again, and lay there. His eyes were looking at the ceiling, but he saw nothing. Tears continued to stream down and collect behind his head. He lay perfectly still. His breathing was steady and for hours, he didn't move.

    Finally, he began to have thoughts. He blinked his eyes and moved his head to see the clock on the nightstand. He checked his phone. He knew that Valencia and Millie had a direct flight to Buenos Aires. But

Tr3.6.6

just in case the eleven-hour flight was interrupted by weather or mechanical issues, he was ready.

In an attempt to get his mind off his unreliable wife, Don sent Mya a message:

"Looking for an ally. Text me when you get this."

He then typed in his number before sending the message. Next, Don skimmed through a few of his favorite pictures posted online of Millie, and then a few of his former girlfriend.

Chapter 18

Sunday, March 26, 2006

Diana Vargas was nine months pregnant and due any day. She procrastinated telling her father, Manuel Vargas, because he didn't offer any man his blessing when it came to Diana. Especially if the man wasn't Dominican and Catholic like him. Don wasn't either of these. In fact, if Manuel found out that Don's grandmother was half Mexican, he would have come after Don. Manuel hated Mexicans.

Manuel also hated what he called half-breeds. Except for Diana. Diana's mother was white. One of many reasons why he felt Diana's husband would have to be Dominican to strengthen the bloodline after his mistake. His words. Diana cried whenever he mentioned that in her presence.

Once Diana finally told Manuel about her pregnancy, he immediately flew to Dallas to spend an entire week with her. When she wasn't in class, she was with him. Manuel lamented about sending

Diana to SMU, and about how he felt he pushed her too hard. She never wanted to be a nurse. She wanted to work for a talent agency in Philadelphia.

Manuel spent the rest of the week pampering Diana, taking her to a local church, and asking for blessings on the baby's behalf. He didn't care too much for the name Diana picked out. Dejahmi. He said it sounded Cuban to him, but he accepted it because Diana loved it.

That Sunday evening, Diana was returning to campus after dropping off her father at the airport. She called her roommate, Bianca Sims, to tell her that instead of going directly back to the apartment, she was going to surprise Don by visiting him at Parkland. He was making up a few hours that he missed during the week. Diana had missed out on a week's worth of alone time with Don. She had to see him.

Around 7:55, Don stepped outside to get some fresh air and check the messages on his phone. Diana had texted him to let him know that her father was on his way to New York. With that news, he called the fourth floor to see if Brenda would allow him to stop by Diana's to surprise her. She allowed him the rest of the night off.

Don drove to the end of Harry Hines Boulevard waiting for the right time to merge into traffic. That's when he noticed Diana's white Jeep waiting to make a left turn onto Harry Hines Boulevard. Don laughed and gestured 'What are you doing?' She laughed and gestured 'Coming to see you.' Don then looked in his rearview to make sure no one was behind him. He needed to back up and make his way back to the parking lot and wait for Diana.

That's when he heard it.

It sounded like an explosion. Instinctively, Don hit his brakes, put his car in park, and jumped out of his car to see if he could locate Diana. From what he observed, Don was able to discern that a dark blue truck crossed over into oncoming traffic and hit Diana head-on at a high rate of speed. Diana's jeep was overturned. Don quickly approached the jeep, which was flipped onto its driver's side, to look for Diana. She was nowhere to be found. Don looked all around and underneath the jeep. Nothing. Don called Diana's name. It had only been two minutes but the chaos made it seem longer than that. Don looked towards Parkland. The crash got the attention of hospital personnel. Help was on the way, but where Diana was remained a mystery.

Don hadn't noticed that traffic had come to a complete halt. People were getting out of their vehicles and converging on the scene. Don saw a large group of people forming five yards from Diana's jeep. Don pushed his way through only to discover that it was the driver of the truck. He reeked of alcohol. Don wanted to kick him in the face.

"Hey! Over here!" a man yelled from outside the crowd. Don followed the voice another five yards to find Diana on the ground next to the sidewalk. Don checked her pulse and her breathing. She was unconscious but alive. He checked her for obvious injuries. He was afraid to move her although he knew how to safely. He just held her hand and called her name until paramedics arrived.

Don called her mother — Cathy Shields. It had been a secret Don kept that both Diana and Cathy appreciated. However, this was not time for secrets. Diana was hurt. Cathy notified every doctor that was on call that night. She didn't know what type of help Diana might have needed but she wanted to be prepared for everything.

It was determined that she landed on her left side and that her hip took most of the direct contact. The doctors immediately looked for obvious signs, external bleeding, and then delivered the baby boy via C-section. Both mother and son were alive but were not in the clear. Unfortunately, Diana was bleeding internally. It went unnoticed for too long. She was pronounced dead at fifteen minutes before midnight. For reasons unexplained, Dejahmi died ten minutes later.

Tr3.6.6

Chapter 19

Saturday, December 15, 2007

Don received a text from Mya.

"Hey. Your message seemed to be a little cryptic. Are you okay?"

"I don't know. Are you busy?" Don texted back.

"No, I got home about an hour ago but I haven't went to bed yet. What's up?" Mya replied.

"You mind if I call?" Don asked.

"No. Call me." Mya texted.

Don stalled for a few minutes before calling. The wait made Mya believe that she somehow missed his call. She kept her phone in her hand and peered at it every twenty seconds until he called. She answered.

"Hello?"

"Hey," Don said.

"Hey, what's on your mind?" Mya asked.

"What isn't?" Don replied.

"Is Millie okay?"

"As far as I know. Her mother took her to Argentina unexpectedly."

"For good?"

"No. Just for a couple of weeks."

"Oh. I bet you miss her."

"Like crazy. That's my baby. She's all I have."

Mya didn't dare mention him having Valencia. Nor did she make a reference to the three of them as a family. She was listening for the moment.

"Have you ever had something you wanted to ask a person even though you were sure you already knew the answer?" Don asked.

"It depends. Like what?" Mya asked.

Just ask me, Mya thought.

"Yeah, I know. I'm being vague. I just wish I had more proof," Don said.

"Proof of what?" Mya asked.

Don hesitated. "I'm looking for an ally, Mya. Can I trust you?"

"I'm looking for one, too. Yes, you can trust me,"

"Okay. I found this note in my wife's car the other day. It was from some guy saying that she should break it off with me because he broke it off with his significant other."

"Do you know the guy?"

"Not by name. At least I think I don't."

"What is his name?"

"I can't remember at the moment. Jalen? Javin?"

"Jarin?"

"Yeah! Yeah that's it. You know him?"

Mya paused before answering. She couldn't figure out if she wanted to be the one to tell him that her ex-boyfriend was the culprit. She was also struggling with the shock of the news.

Valencia is the one that Lisa was referring to?

She couldn't be for sure. As soon as Lisa indicated she knew the woman Jarin was cheating with, Mya hung up the phone. She hadn't talked to Lisa since then.

"Hello?" Don said.

"I'm here," Mya replied.

"Oh okay. I thought I lost you. So, what do you think I should do?" Don asked.

"That seems like pretty convincing evidence to me," Mya said.

"Yeah, but I need more. I want to be able to back her into the corner with it."

"And once you get your answer, what do you plan to do?"

"I'm getting a divorce."

"Just like that?"

"Yeah. It's been over. I can't stand it when she tries to hug or kiss me. Lay beside me. All she likes to do is drink. I focus most of my energy on Millie."

"Then why wait for more evidence? Why not just divorce her anyway?" Mya asked.

"I'm looking for an inevitable way out. Besides, it's not that simple," Don said.

Chapter 20

After Diana was laid to rest, Don lost all motivation to continue pursuing higher education. He didn't really have a passion for nursing; he just knew it meant job security. Diana was his sole motivation to remain in the program. They had been dating since their freshmen year, and although they didn't spend every available moment together, Don was sure that he loved her. Diana loved him more and he knew that. That's why he stayed in the program for so long. He would have completed it had Diana not been killed.

 Cathy tried to convince Don that Diana's death was all the more reason to complete the program. However, Don knew Diana better than Cathy did. Cathy got pregnant during her college years while vacationing in Miami. When she notified Manuel that she was giving up the baby for adoption, he insisted on raising his daughter himself. Diana's father related the story to her when she was in high school. Thus, Diana used it as an excuse to put her dreams on hold and pursue a more demanding career right before her mother's eyes. Diana didn't intentionally get pregnant, but she did nothing to prevent it from happening. The pregnancy, though, was the exclamation point on proving to her mother that she could have been in Diana's life. Had none of that taken place, Diana would have loved to work at Reinhard Model and Talent Agency in Philadelphia.

Therefore, Don immediately withdrew from SMU and moved to Philly in order to live out Diana's dream for a while. Initially, Don was nothing more than a gopher. An errand boy. He worked under a casting director slash television network liaison named Tom Lediner, whose yelling was only outmatched by his halitosis. People often kept their distance from him, but no one could recall which came first — the halitosis, the distance, or the yelling.

Regardless, the high-stress environment kept Tom with ulcers and irritable bowels. Thus, he often needed his prescription of sulfasalazine picked up from the CVS on Chestnut Street. He didn't care for any other pharmacy because (according to him) the CVS on chestnut was the only pharmacy that understood the seriousness of condition. The CVS knew him so well that they allowed Tom's assistants to come pick up his medication for him. That's how Don met Valencia.

Valencia had been working at CVS as a pharmacy technician for a year before Don walked in to retrieve Tom's prescription. She had been living with her cousin in Philly for four years and had completed her schooling at Community College of Philadelphia. She hadn't really partied as a young adult mainly because she was determined to make enough money to move her mother from Argentina into a home in the United States one day.

Valencia was intrigued by Don the second she met him. She made small talk with him. She noticed that he didn't have an east coast accent. She was also surprised that he didn't attempt any pickup lines like most of the customers she encountered. She was especially creeped out by the customers who came to pick up their prescriptions for erectile dysfunction, venereal diseases, and psychotropics that yet promised her a good time if she went home with them. It seemed that they assumed that Valencia was too pretty to know what the mediation was for. Yet, Don was nothing like those guys.

By the time Don was ready to return to work, Valencia had convinced Don to accompany her for a night out to celebrate her twenty-second birthday. Don wouldn't be twenty-two until later that year.

April twenty-second was a Saturday. Don quickly noticed that he was the only guy formerly invited out with Valencia, her cousin, and two of her co-workers. Don limited himself to two drinks, while Valencia and the other women experimented taking shots out of one another's bosoms. Valencia often tried to keep Don involved by licking salt off his neck as she took a shot. Don was somewhat put-off by Valencia's wild behavior but appreciated the temporary distraction. One of Valencia's co-workers made sure that was short-lived.

"How come you don't have a girlfriend?"

Don felt as if the world stopped to wait for his answer. He didn't hear the music, the group of women giggling and teasing him about being a player, nothing. He just felt the stares.

"Excuse me," Don said as he got up from the table. But he wasn't headed to the restroom. He went straight for one of the exits.

Valencia made it outside to see the cab he entered drive away. Given that he wasn't from there, there was only one place that he could go. Don had given Valencia his address earlier that night so she could give him directions to the club. He took a cab anyway to prevent getting lost.

Valencia arrived at the sublet apartment he was leasing (on a month-to-month basis) shortly after he did. Don wasn't in the mood for company. He'd rather drink away his misery and mourn the loss of his girlfriend and child. He had no business being out with another woman so soon, but when Valencia showed up at his place, he felt compelled to tell her the whole story. Valencia held him close and tenderly kissed him on the forehead. By the time she left his place at noon the next day, they had sex four times.

Valencia started spending the night at Don's apartment more often. Don allowed it because he needed the company. Valencia, on the other hand was starting to get attached. Both would agree that the sex was great.

Two weeks into it, Don made it clear that he wasn't ready for a relationship. Valencia had already declared them a couple to her friends at work. When Don tried to end it, Valencia threatened suicide. She decided that she loved Don and she didn't want to lose him. Don agreed to see how things worked out between them.

Soon after his grandfather was murdered in Dallas, he allowed Diana's dream to die with her. He told Valencia that he was moving back home. Valencia didn't leave Philly until a month later when she found out she was pregnant. Don moved her into his mother's house shortly before they moved into their apartment at Amesbury Parc.

Cathy pulled a few strings to get Valencia hired on at Parkland.

Emilia was born in April the following year. They married two months later. And Don has been stuck with Valencia ever since.

Chapter 21

Saturday, December 15, 2007

Mya fully understood the story of Don and Valencia, but now she wanted to help him get to the bottom of this cheating thing. Well, mostly it was for selfish reasons. Although she wasn't with Jarin anymore, it hurt her to know that he was willing to throw away their history for some foreign floozy from Argentina. Her words.

She didn't want to give Jarin the wrong impression by asking him directly. That could imply that she still cared and may be looking for an excuse to be in his company again. Mya also knew that his friends would cover for him, so she couldn't play them for information. The only person she could rely on was Lisa, but they hadn't talked in a week. Lisa knew a guy that could get answers for them.

Mya texted Lisa instead of calling her. She explained that she needed the information for a friend, but Lisa already knew it was for Don. Lisa came back within minutes with a temporary password that would allow Don to log into Valencia's Facebook account. Lisa explained, though, that the hacker was having difficulty getting into Jarin's account, but he would keep trying.

While she waited for Lisa to text her back with another password, Mya called Don with what she already had.

"Are you sure you want to do this?" Mya asked.

"Yeah," Don said. "Thank you"

"No problem," Mya said. "Let me know what you find out."

Chapter 22

Sunday, December 16, 2007

Carlita contacted Don Saturday afternoon to let him know that Valencia and Emilia were okay. Carlita knew that her sister would make Don worry to death as a way of punishing him for not coming with her. Although her mother blamed Don for Valencia's episodes of self-mutilation before she fell ill, Carlita knew better. She didn't know the whole story between Don and Valencia, but Carlita did know that Valencia started cutting herself at the age of eleven. Juanita, their mother, turned a blind eye to it and planted a poisonous seed (of Don mentally and physically abusing Valencia) amongst the rest of the family.

Through Carlita, Don had managed to set up a time for Valencia to call him. He claimed it was important so Valencia called him at two in the afternoon. Central time zone.

"Hi, Don-Don," Valencia said.

"How's Emilia?" Don asked.

"She's good," Valencia said.

"How's your mother?" Don asked.

"Not so good, but she could be worse. She no say my name. How are you? You miss me?"

"I know, Valencia."

"You know what?"

"I know about you and Brian."

"What about him?

"I know about Brian, I know about Rob. And I know about Rich."

"Don-Don..."

"It's fine. Just know that when you come back, I want a divorce."

"Baby—"

"Don't baby me," Don said. He spoke in a really calm manner, with no voice inflection at all. He was a stone.

"Don-Don..." Valencia pleaded. She began to cry. Don was unmoved.

"Don't call me that either."

"Adonis, listen, I-I no cheat. I no remember! I—"

"You don't remember the flower either, huh?"

"What flower?"

"The flower in the glove compartment of your car. The one that came with a note from Jarin."

"Okay, that not for me. I promise! That for other girl in my car."

"Who? Who else would be in your car?" Don asked.

"Lisa! She tell you. She take my car for dinner," Valencia explained.

"Who is the guy?"

"He football player. Game changer, they say. He not for me."

Watts? Wait a minute...Isn't that Mya's boyfriend? Don thought.

"Never mind that. You've done enough. I'm done," Don said.

"No wait! I tell you, I tell you! Please," Valencia said.

"I'm listening," Don said.

"You have to believe me," Valencia said.

"Just say it so I can go."

"It's Rich. He-he rape me!"

Tr3.6.6

Chapter 23

Don didn't buy Valencia's story, but he didn't completely dismiss it. At the moment, though, he felt the need to pass on the information he had and tie up a few loose ends with Mya. He texted her; requesting that she call at her first available moment. She called him immediately.

"Hey." Don said.

"Hey. Is everything okay?" Mya asked.

"Who is Jarin to you?" Don asked. His question made Mya go on the defensive.

"No one. He used to be my boyfriend, but that ended. For good this time," Mya explained.

"How long ago?"

"The night I kissed you." Mya knew how it sounded. It was as if she broke up with Jarin for Don. She hoped that it would put Don on the defensive. It didn't. Don believed in coincidences.

"I see. Well, I have bad news and I have bad news. Which would you like to hear?" Don asked.

Mya was nervous due to the line of questioning that preceded the statement he just made.

"Any good news at all?" Mya asked.

"Umm…I don't think Jarin and Valencia ever slept together," Don said.

What? I swear that was going to be the bad news, Mya thought.

"Okay then, what is the difference between the bad news and the bad news, as you say?" Mya asked.

"Some for me. Some for you," Don said.

"You first," Mya said.

"As we already know, my wife is a whore. But, what we didn't know is that my wife was or is sleeping with my friend Rich."

"Oh no. I'm sorry to hear that. Are you okay?"

"I've taken it in stride. Still processing it. But I'm more concerned about how you will take your bad news."

Mya sighed heavily. "Let's hear it."

"The note I found from Jarin wasn't for Val. It was for your friend Lisa."

Chapter 24

"Having any luck with Jarin's account?" Mya asked.

As soon as she had ended her conversation with Don, Mya called Lisa. It took a while for her to gather her thoughts and composure. Don wouldn't let her off the phone until she promised not to do anything crazy and to call him back by ten that night. She wasn't crying audibly. It was the dead silence that indicated to Don that she didn't take the news well. She and Lisa had made fast friends. They vacationed together twice and were planning a third before Mya found out about Lisa keeping Jarin's secret. But, Mya was near forgiving Lisa. Well, that was before Don dropped this bombshell on her. Lisa was truly a backstabbing, phony, two-faced bitch. Her words.

"Uh, well, I don't know. He hadn't said anything else about it," Lisa said.

"I wasn't talking about him. I asked about you," Mya said.

"I told you, I have a guy that does it for me," Lisa replied.

"Sure you do," Mya said.

"What are you implying, Mya?"

"Let's just say the cat is out of the bag."

"What?"

"Too cliché for you? Okay. I'll try the more direct approach. Look, bitch. I know that there is no guy. There's never been. But, you know who does know a guy? My dad. And his guy knows that you've been quite the little hacker since you've learned computer programming. You even managed to change your high school grades and your A-C-T score," Mya explained.

Lisa grew quiet. She paused before answering.

"What do you want?"

"Nothing. But you obviously want what I have. Correction, had. I know about you and Jarin. And you know what? At this point, I don't care. You should have been woman enough, though, to tell Steve. Who, by the way, thinks you're a goddess for some odd reason. But you're a coward and apparently, a habitual liar."

"So, what now? Are you going to report me?" Lisa asked.

"Not at all. But if I were you, I would stay far away from me. In fact, I would transfer, because I wouldn't want me to be reminded about this whole ordeal," Mya said.

"How am I going to get accepted to another school this late into the program?" Lisa asked.

"Oh I'm sure, that with your special set of skills, you'll find a way," Mya said right before ending the call.

Chapter 25

Monday, December 17, 2007 — 12:16 AM

"Hello," Don answered.

"It's me," Mya said.

"I know it's you. I have your number saved in my phone," Don said.

"Oh. I'm late," Mya said.

"Which late?"

"What?"

"What do you mean by you're late?"

"I'm late calling. I was supposed to call by ten."

"Oh. I thought you meant something else. I was gonna say that you should be telling the guy that caused you to be late."

"For real?" Mya laughed.

"For real, for real. Last I checked you can't get pregnant over the phone," Don said.

"How about from kissing?" Mya asked.

"That either," Don said.

Mya laughed again. Within a minute of talking to him, she already felt better. She regretted not calling him sooner.

"I almost didn't call. I thought you would be sleep," Mya said.

"Not quite. I'm just laying here. Relaxing. You okay? What happened to you?" Don asked.

"I fell asleep. I guess I was exhausted."

"Oh. Then go to sleep."

"No, I want to talk to you."

"Ok. Talk."

"Give me something to talk about."

"Really? I'm supposed to be listening. I'm great at that."

"Just pick something."

"Okay, okay. Um…do you have any siblings?"

"One. An older sister. She's much older."

"Like thirty years older?"

"No, half that."

"Oh. So, you were unexpected."

"Pretty much. How about you?"

"I was planned, thank you very much."

"No silly. I meant do you have siblings?"

"Nope. Not that I know of."

"Oh. Where did you grow up?" Mya asked.

"In Dallas," Don said.

"I know that much."

"Oh. On Highland."

"I grew up in Highland Park, too! I don't remember you in high school. Did you go to Highland Park High?"

"Whoa! I grew up on Highland Village Drive. South Oak Cliff? I'm sure you've heard of it on the news."

Mya was somewhat embarrassed. "Oh. My bad."

"Yeah, I'm a project kid. No worries, I get my rabies shots. You won't catch it from me," Don joked.

"I don't think like that."

"Relax. Somebody has to grow up rich. We're both minorities. Kinda. What's your ethnicity?"

"My dad is half white, half black. My mom is Samoan."

"Damn."

"What does that mean?"

"I'm in love with your gene pool."

Mya laughed. "Really? That's all it takes?"

"What can I say? I'm a breeder," Don said.

That last comment caused Mya to imagine what it would be like to "breed" with Don.

"What's that music in the background?" Mya asked in an attempt to change her own thoughts.

"It's the radio," Don said.

"Yeah, but what song?" Mya asked.

"*With You* by Chris Brown," Don said.

"That same song was on the last time we talked on the phone. And the time before that."

"Well it's not like I play it when I know you're on the phone. It's the radio, not my laptop."

"You sure?"

"Tune in to KISS one-oh-six-one."

She did. Sure enough, it was playing.

"I really like this song," Mya said.

"Yeah. I like it, too," Don said.

"Why do you like it?"

"Because it's a good song. I like the lyrics. Why do you like it?"

"I like the lyrics too. But, now I like it because it reminds me of you."

A sinking feeling came over Don. "What about me?"

"I don't know, just you. Talking to you on the phone. I think it's a sign."

"A sign from whom?"

"I don't know, maybe fate."

"You see, that's the thing. Everybody seems to talk about fate as if he or she or it has the right to choose our destinies. Consider me a rebel. Why would a beautiful, independent woman, like you, want to listen to fate?" Don asked.

"I can't say. All I know is that it was here before us and it will be here when we're gone. Maybe he or she or it knows something we don't and sends us a message in the form of a sign," Mya explained.

"A sign of what?"

"That I should be doing something."

"Something like what?" I'm not sure. All I know is that I should be doing it with you."

"Doing it, huh?"

Mya laughed. "Nothing gets past you, does it?"

"Not often," Don said.

"So humble."

"You like it."

Mya didn't understand why she liked it, but she did. At least for the moment. She was hoping there was more to him that she hadn't discovered.

Only time will tell, Mya thought.

Chapter 26

Monday, December 24, 2007

Mya and Don talked on the phone every night for a week. They hadn't attempted to meet up. They didn't plan any dates. They made a game of listening to the radio together and counting the number of times "With You" came on during their conversation. The record for one conversation was fourteen times between three radio stations. They wouldn't talk when it came on. It was as if the song spoke for the both of them. They also came up with a game called "Hard Question Time" where they could ask as many personal questions as they wanted in one hour. The game was always at the same time every night — from eleven to midnight.

The two developed a few inside jokes. For instance, Don teased Mya for choosing orange and purple as her two favorite colors. Since neither of those are primary colors, Don often said that Mya was a second-class citizen with a first-class pedigree. Mya would tease that the reason why Don was so mean was because he had a toddler penis. Don claimed it was true, but Mya assumed the opposite. Don would rib Mya about her sister actually being her mother and claimed that her whole family was lying to her. Mya didn't think that was as funny as the other jokes. She secretly considered it a possibility since she was the only one with hazel eyes in her family; a fact that Don was unaware of.

Between work and long conversations with Mya, Don didn't think of Valencia at all. He missed Emilia daily, but Mya served as a distraction. She kept him focused on Emilia's return rather than how long she had been away.

Christmas Eve at Mya's home meant stuffy company, a lot of fake laughs, and forced smiles. Christmas Eve for Don just meant a day off. He spent the day visiting his mother and grandmother. Other than that, Don didn't do much. Don knew that Mya's family was the traditional type and he probably wouldn't hear from Mya. If he did, it would be late and by then she would be exhausted. But, he was wrong.

"What are you doing?" Mya texted.

"Breathing. Texting this beautiful lady." Don texted back.

"Really? Do I know her?"

"Nope. But I really like her a lot."

"How much is a lot?"

"Borderline more than like."

"Interesting because I borderline more than like a guy I know." Mya texted.

"Really? Maybe we could double date some time." Don texted.

"I'm available tonight."

"So am I."

"Where should we meet?"

"How about Olivella's on Mcfarland Blvd?"

"I love Italian!"

Tr3.6.6

"My lady friend does too." Don replied.
"Lol we're silly. I'll see you at 7:30." Mya texted.

Chapter 27

After dinner, Don and Mya talked for a short while in the parking lot in front of Mya's Lexus Sedan. They shared an awkward hug and a telling stare, but no kiss. No one dared to make the first move. Don returned to his vehicle and drove away first. Mya was already in hers, but she stayed put. She needed time to process her wandering thoughts.

Ten minutes later, she called Don.

"Hello," Don answered.

"What am I to you?" Mya asked.

Don sighed then looked at the clock. It was only 9:46.

"It's not hard question time. You're not playing fair," Don said.

"Meet me," Mya said.

"Where?"

"The Highland Hotel on Mockingbird Lane."

"Never been. Sounds expensive."

"Just meet me."

"Is this a good idea?"

"It's not what you think. Just get here."

"Now?"

"Yes. Don't change clothes. I want to be able to find you in a crowd."

Mya ended the call. Don stalled for twenty minutes before leaving his apartment. He didn't want to appear desperate to see her.

Just get here? She must have gone straight there. Maybe she planned it before we even had dinner.

Don arrived at the hotel shortly before 10:30. He had never been to the hotel before. He felt totally out of place. He couldn't find another person wearing jeans at all. Granted, his jeans weren't baggy; but they were still jeans.

As soon as Don stepped inside, Mya grabbed him by the arm. He relaxed once he realized it was her. They walked hand-in-hand as she guided him to the elevators and didn't say a word until they were inside the elevator alone.

"I thought you might not come," Mya said.

"I'm never on time for a party," Don said.

"Good to know. Next time I'll tell you an hour in advance," Mya said.

"Don't tell me that. I'll use it against you and start being two hours late," Don said.

Mya laughed. "There's no winning with you, is there?"

"It depends on what you're trying to win. What's this about?"

Mya stepped in front of Don and faced him. "I need something from you."

"You have to give to get in this life," Don said.

"What do you want?" Mya asked.

"Nothing more than what you're trying to offer," Don replied.

The elevator opened at the ninth floor. Mya led the way to the room. Don didn't know what to expect, but his heart grew faint with anticipation; knowing that Mya had something in mind.

"Here we are. Room nine-eighteen," Mya said.

"Wait a minute," Don said. Mya wore a perplexed look on her face. "Where on this sign do you see nine-eighteen?"

"There's a nine, a one, and an eight all in sequence," Mya said as if she was teaching a child.

"Ah, but in the English language, we pronounce it nine-hundred-eighteen. You Texans are lazy," Don said.

"No, nine-eighteen is the same thing."

"No, it is not."

"Well tonight this is room nine-eighteen."

"Okay then let's make it official." Don reached into his pocket and pulled out his keys.

"What are you doing?" Mya asked with a curious grin on her face.

"You'll see," Don said. He used a key to scratch a jagged line between the nine and the one.

"What is that?" Mya asked.

"It's a dash. Now you can rightfully call this room nine-eighteen," Don explained.

"That's not a dash, that's a crooked line!"

"Yeah to match your crooked lingo."

They laughed briefly. Mya looked at Don and touched his face to get his full attention.

"It's not what you think," Mya said softly.

"How do you know what I think?" Don asked.

"Who am I to you?" Mya asked ignoring his question. Don looked away then back at Mya. She turned to the door, opened it, and held out her hand to Don. Don grabbed her hand and stepped to the door.

Tr3.6.6

Chapter 28

"Let's make a pact," Mya said.

"I'm listening." Don replied.

"This room is a no lie zone. In here, we have no secrets. We can be us without reservation. In here, we're allowed to dream, to laugh, to cry, to be whomever we want. We're safe here. You're safe here," Mya said.

Don took his eyes off the room and looked at Mya. "If this is Neverland, you must be Tinkerbell."

Mya laughed. "Must you make a joke about everything?"

"I must say, I'm a little old to be Peter Pan," Don said.

"Don..." Mya whined.

"You're funny when you pout," Don said.

"Do we have a pact?"

"No gimmicks? No commitment clauses?"

"No gimmicks."

Don noted that she didn't agree to no commitments.

"Okay. We have a pact."

Mya walked him into the room far enough to allow the door to close behind him.

"Who am I to you?" Mya inquired.

"Who do you think you are?" Don asked.

"Something like a girlfriend," Mya said hopeful.

Don shook his head and tapped his chest.

"What does that mean?" Mya asked.

"You're not my girlfriend," Don said.

"Then what?"

Don met Mya's worried look with a warm smile. He took both of her hands in his and shortened the gap between them by taking one step closer. Don then said,

"You're my heart."

Mya immediately became teary-eyed. She tried to speak but her voice cracked and squealed as if Don was the surgeon that told her that her whole family died on the operating table. Of course, that never happened. Don tried consoling her by hugging her and holding her close. She tried to hug him back but her arms wouldn't cooperate. She was trying to tell him that she had never heard that before, but the words wouldn't quite come out. All she could do was sob. Don picked her up and placed her on the bed.

As Mya lay on her back covering her face, Don sat next to her and played with her hair.

"Hey," Don said gently. "Hey, Mya…stop it…stop crying…for me."

Mya finally gathered herself and took a deep breath.

"There you go," Don said. "I thought you were a lot tougher than that."

"I am," Mya said between sniffs and wiping her eyes. "You just surprised me. I don't like surprises." She attempted to briefly laugh through the tears.

"Yeah you do," Don said.

"You're right. I do, but this was a total blind-side," Mya said.

"I doubt that. You're more perceptive than you think you are."

"Tell me what you mean when you call me that."

"I think you already know."

"Tell me anyway."

"I love you, Mya."

"I knew it," Mya said but her words were barely discernable because she was crying again.

Don lay beside Mya on his side and gently stroked her cheek with his finger. He then turned Mya's head toward him.

"No more crying, okay?" Don said.

Mya nodded, but it took a while for her eyes to comply.

"Why would you cry when I tell you that I love you?" Don asked.

Mya took a deep breath, "Because I...I...I..."

Don kissed her. Mya tried to tell him. She couldn't form the words. She wanted to. Maybe she could later. His kiss calmed her. She had been waiting for him to kiss her since the first time she kissed him. Don attempted to pull away, but Mya sensed it and threw her arms around his neck. Don managed to pull away just enough to break off the kissing.

"Easy, Mya. I'm not going anywhere," Don whispered.

"Promise?" Mya asked.

"Promise," Don said softly.

Mya kissed him and went to the bathroom to wash her face. Don removed his shoes and relaxed on the bed. He knew he had to be solid for the both of them. He was comfortable around Mya. Maybe too comfortable. But, even without Mya designating the room as a safe zone, he felt safe around her no matter where they were. As long as they were together. Don still had plenty of walls he could put between him and Mya. He would rather not. Mya was his confidant, friend, and heroine. He had hope that she could save him from the madness known as his life. Maybe it was unrealistic expectations but, as Mya said, he was allowed to dream.

Mya returned to the bed in a perky manner. She was smiling from embarrassment hoping that Don couldn't fathom the difference. He could. He was a great reader of character. Mya loved looking into his eyes but found it difficult that night. She needed Don's assurance that they would be fine as a couple despite him being legally married. Common sense would tell her that she would encounter problems. But, who listens to common sense these days? Her words. Her heart made it clear to her that this was the only thing that made sense. A troubled life with Don was better than a carefree life without him. Also her words. Maybe, though, just maybe this could work. In room nine-eighteen, Mya was allowed to dream.

Don invited her to lie in his arms. Instead, she lay next to him on her left side, facing away from him. She then pulled his right arm around her around her and nestled against his body. She closed her eyes and took a deep breath. She interlocked her fingers with his and kissed his hand.

"Don," Mya said.

"I know, Mya. I know." Don replied.

Mya relaxed; content that Don understood. She couldn't help the silent tears though. He just knew what to say. She couldn't decide if he was the perfect guy, the smoothest talker she'd ever met, or a combination of the two. For the moment, she was happy with this one thought:

He knows.

Chapter 29

The next morning, Mya was already awake. She was seated next to a sleeping Don, watching his chest rise and fall. She wanted to invite him to her parent's house, but thought better of it. Instead, she decided to go for another first with Don. Mya placed her hand on Don's chest. He didn't start. Given that he was only wearing boxers, she decided to find another way to wake him. She allowed her hand to wander past his abs, his waistline, and settle upon the stiff bulge she felt behind her overnight. She gave into the sudden urge to squeeze it to get a good feel.

Damn.

Don still didn't react. Mya leaned over to kiss Don as she massaged his dick.

"Rah!" Don belted out as he grabbed Mya around the shoulders. Mya squealed then giggled as she froze in place and fell into him.

"You were pretending this whole time? "Mya asked.

"You were enjoying yourself. Why would I interrupt you?" Don replied.

"I was trying to get your attention," Mya said.

"It seems you already have," Don said suggestively.

Mya finally released her hold, sat up and stood next to the bed.

"Join me," Mya said.

Don noticed that she was wearing only a towel.

"Bring your friend with you," Mya said before scampering off to the shower. Don followed closely behind to get a view of her stepping into the shower. He was a second too late. Mya laughed. She could hear him barge in. She knew what he was up to. Mya turned on the shower and stood under the showerhead. Don peeked his head around the glass sliding door to get a clearer view of Mya's naked body. Mya splashed him with water.

"Get in here before the water gets cold," Mya demanded.

"In a place like this, the water never gets cold," Don replied.

"Okay then, before my fingers get all wrinkly," Mya said.

"Is that a word?" Don asked.

"Of course."

"I'll go check."

"Don…"

"Ah, the magic whine."

"You make me whine."

Don undressed and joined Mya underneath the water.

"Is that better?" Don asked.

Mya handed Don a soapy loofa, turned around, and pulled her hair over her shoulder.

"Do you mind?" Mya asked.

"Not at all," Don said as he went to work gently washing Mya's back. He couldn't help but follow the suds with his eyes as they traveled down her back and cascaded over her luscious curves. Don managed to fight through his urges, but he couldn't control his thoughts. Unfortunately, the same thing that separates southern Oklahoma from northern Texas separated Mya and Don. The Red River. But, Don was content with the touching, the kissing, and the showering. For now. He figured that night served as the grownup version of show and tell and that things could only advance from there.

Neither of them brought a change of clothes, so they dressed in the clothes from the night before. That meant that Don would shower again when he got to his apartment. He was a hygiene freak.

Mya decided to memorialize the night with a photo. She grabbed her digital camera from her purse and hurriedly found Don in front of the mirror in the bathroom. Mya sought the best angle in the yellow, incandescent lighting. She finally settled on pinning Don against a near wall with her body. She stood on her toes in order to be cheek to cheek with Don. She supported herself with her left arm around Don's shoulder while she extended the camera away from her with her right hand to snap the picture.

Mya had to make an appearance at home, so the two decided to skip breakfast. Don kissed Mya goodbye and left the hotel before her. Mya pinched herself (when she was all alone) to see if she was dreaming. She knew it was childish, but Adonis proved to be the perfect gentleman and had thus lived up to his mother's expectations. That was something Mya didn't deem possible for any man. She had been striking out since high school, which caused her to lower her expectations. She had allowed herself to make assumptions about Don before that night, which she was embarrassed to admit. She had been proven wrong. And at that moment, she was allowing herself to dream.

Mrs. Mya Lane? Mrs. Adonis Lane? Mrs. Don Lane. Yeah, Mrs. Don Lane.

Chapter 30

Wednesday, January 2, 2008

Mya spent the rest of the holiday season with her family but managed to ensure that Don's voice was the last voice she heard before she went to bed. She still hadn't got around to telling Don that she loved him, but it would come…eventually. She didn't go into detail about what her family did on their outings. She was slightly embarrassed about being a senator's daughter. She didn't want Don to feel as if she was out of touch with reality and privileged. Of course, if he were politically inclined, he would have seen Mya's face displayed on CNN next to her father's at Charity events, orphanages, and homeless shelters in the Dallas area.

The new year meant a new beginning for Don. He was determined not to allow Valencia to make him feel that he had to stay anymore. If he was going to be in a relationship, it was because he wanted to. That's what he had with Mya. No pressure. Freedom. Genuine interest. Honesty and trust. Things he didn't have with Valencia. With that new attitude in mind, he spent the second day of the new year cleaning out items that would cause Valencia to believe that they still had a home together. He took every picture that he was in off the walls. He destroyed every type of greeting card he gave her. He moved all of his casual clothes to the closet in Emilia's room.

For Don, though, these measures were not drastic enough. He wanted something that she would notice the second she walked in the door. He wanted her to know that he was serious and that their time together was up. Therefore, Don sold the living room furniture to a consignment store including the television. They never hosted any dinners or gatherings at their apartment. They weren't friends with other couples. His mother never visited him there because she could sense the tension and strife between the two of them. Therefore, Don didn't see the point of having the furniture anymore.

Don didn't specify what he did when he talked to Mya that night. Only that he had taken the first big step towards a clean break.

"How do you feel about it?" Mya asked.

"I feel it's about time," Don said.

"When is she due back?" Mya asked.

"Tomorrow."

Chapter 31

Thursday, January 3, 2008

Don made it to the gate of the airport thirty minutes early. He wanted to get used to the ambience as to not excite at the sight of Valencia. He noticed that joy proved to be contagious when others on the same flight were greeted by their loved ones. He wanted no part of that. On the other hand, seeing Millie was nearly a party any day of the week. Further, Don wanted the changes in the apartment to be one devastating shock after another. Therefore, he would have to be slightly more than cordial when greeting Valencia. Just slightly.

The flight arrived seven minutes early. People were starting to file into the terminal. Families began embracing their loved ones and handing over flowers. One guy even proposed to a woman carrying a laptop. A little girl was waving a sign that read, 'Welcome home Daddy'. Other than the 'C' being backwards, Don thought the act was cute and heartwarming. The flow of exiting passengers slowed to a trickle. No sign of Val or Millie. Don was starting to think they didn't come back.

Suddenly, Valencia appeared carrying a bundled Millie. Don saw Millie, but there was something about Valencia that caught his attention. It was the dress. It was the same purple dress she wore on her twenty-second birthday. Don was pretty sure that the shawl around her shoulders was the one from that night too. One thing was for sure, Valencia looked beautiful.

Don tried to steel his feelings. However, his disdainful thoughts were replaced with thoughts of that night. How kind she was. How she seemed to care. How she came through for him at a time when he was mourning. Valencia was only twenty feet away. Don snapped to attention and offered to take Millie out of her arms. During the exchange, Don and Valencia made eye contact and, out of impulse, shared a kiss similar to their first one.

"Hey," Don said to Valencia.

"So, you *did* miss me," Valencia said to Don and smiled.

Don offered no response. Instead, he turned to Millie, who, now in his arms, was smiling hugely at the sight of her Daddy.

"Hey, Daddy's baby! Hey, my Boobie! Did you miss Daddy? Daddy missed you so much!" Don said while making his way to baggage claim.

Don and Valencia didn't carry on an upbeat conversation. There was tension, but not the bad kind. Don had lost focus and misled Valencia by making eyes with her during red lights, kissing her, and holding her hand while driving left-handed. He also wore a familiar seductive smile that Valencia hadn't seen in a while. Val had a notion that the night would end with sex for sure. However, when they were within a block of their apartment, Don's demeanor changed. His smile faded. He no longer looked in Valencia's direction. Valencia just figured he saw a cop car and decided it was best to focus on the road. Don didn't trust cops.

They arrived. Valencia insisted on dragging one of the suitcases up to their second-floor apartment while Don balanced the other one and Millie at the same time. She didn't want Don to make a second trip back to the car. She intended to keep him in the bedroom all night. Val unlocked the door and pushed the door open so Don could go first. He left the luggage in the middle of the living room floor and continued to Millie's room. Valencia stepped inside and paused just inside the front door.

"Don-Don?" Valencia asked. Don could hear the concern in her voice.

"The bedroom hasn't moved. I'll be sleeping in Millie's room tonight. Sleep tight," Don said before entering Millie's room and closing the door behind him.

Valencia fell to her knees and sobbed.

It really is over, Valencia thought.

Chapter 32

Friday, January 4, 2008

"I miss you," Mya said to her lunch date across the table. It was Don. They decided to meet for barbeque at Peggy Sue on Snider Plaza.

"I miss you." Don said between bites of brisket.

"Prove it," Mya said.

"How so?" Don asked.

"Meet me tonight."

"I can't. I got Millie."

"Aw. How is she?"

"Bubbly as ever."

"When can I babysit?"

Don looked up from his plate of food at Mya. He was looking to see if there was any hint that she was joking.

"That's quite a task for someone who doesn't have kids of their own," Don said.

"I'm great with kids," Mya said.

"You think so?" Don asked.

"Yep," Mya said confidently.

"How many nieces and nephews do you have?"

"None."

"How many of your friends have kids?"

"None."

"How many of your cousins have kids?"

"I have a cousin that's prego. Does that count?"

"No."

"Then, none."

"How many times have you changed a diaper at Parkland?"

"Twice. Only because Brenda doesn't allow me to handle the preemies."

"Mm hm. Interview over," Don said.

"So?" Mya asked.

"So, what?"

"How did I do?"

"Oh. You failed."

"What? Based off what criteria?" she asked with a smile.

"Lack of experience!" Don said playfully.

"You suck."

"No, I eat."

Mya picked up on the sexual innuendo. "Prove it."

Don looked up at Mya again. This time Mya wore a grin.

"In due time. In the meantime, how bad do you want this babysitting job?"

"I would really like a shot at it."

"I may have a way to get you hands-on experience. But you really have to want it."

"I do but—"

"No buts. Do you trust me or not?" Don asked.

Mya sighed then smiled. She squinted at him skeptically.

"I trust you." Mya said.

"Good. After we're done here, go home and pack you an overnight bag."

"Why?"

"You're spending the night with me and Millie."

Chapter 33

It was about two-thirty. Trepidation kept Mya from knocking. Mya stood outside apartment 211 waiting for Don to open the door. She noticed that she was standing next to a bedroom window that was perpendicular to the front door. She couldn't tell if there were curtains on the window or not. All she could see was the blinds and blinds weren't enough to conceal the silhouette of a person outside the window. To Mya, that meant if Valencia were in there she would likely open the door to see who was standing outside the window. That's why Mya sent Don a text from the parking lot. She expected him to meet her at the door. After what seemed like ten minutes, the door opened.

"Hey." It was Don.

"Hey," Mya said quietly. She didn't know if Valencia was home or not.

"Sorry to keep you waiting. I was in the middle of a diaper change when you texted me," Don explained.

Mya sent the text at 2:27. Mya looked at her phone. It was only 2:29.

"That's okay. I didn't wait long," Mya said.

Don stepped aside and gestured for her to come in. Mya stopped just inside the door. She didn't go any further hoping that the room nearest the front door was where they were headed. The empty living room made the walk to the far room seem like an exodus. She would be exposed with nothing to protect her from Valencia's wrath in the form of flying shoes, sharp objects, bullets…the list goes on. Her words.

"Millie's room is this way," Don said.

As Mya feared, it was the far room. Just before they reached the bedroom door, Mya could hear the other bedroom door open. She was afraid to look. It was Valencia. Don looked over at Valencia. She was wearing one of Don's t-shirts from college that she often wore to bed and a worried look on her face. Don gave her a warning glare. Valencia reluctantly closed the door. By then, Mya was seated on the bed in Millie's room. Don closed the door behind him and took Millie out of her crib. He carried Millie over to Mya.

"I want you to meet somebody, Millie," Don said cheerfully.

He then handed Millie over to Mya.

Mya stood Millie in her lap.

"Hi, Emilia! Hi, beautiful! How are you?" Mya went on.

Don observed how Millie reacted to Mya. Millie flailed her arms in excitement. Don could tell Emilia liked her new friend. Millie looked to her daddy, who was reclining next to Mya propped up on one arm, as if she wanted to know if he approved of Mya too.

Don smiled and Millie went back to cooing and listening to Mya tell her how beautiful she was.

Don received a text from Valencia.

"Why is she here?"

He ignored it, but Mya didn't.

"Are you sure about this?" Mya asked Don.

"I can handle her. You just focus on Millie," Don said.

Mya nodded.

"Hey, Millie. Let's show Mya how well you can walk," Don said.

"She can walk?" Mya asked.

"She can, but she'll only takes a few steps before she gets scared and plops down on her bottom," Don said.

"You can walk Millie? I wanna see," Mya said.

Don sat on the floor and instructed Mya to sit five feet in front of him with Millie in her lap. With Millie facing Don, Mya helped Millie to stand while she supported herself on Mya's hands. With outstretched arms, Don encouraged Millie to come to him. Millie did. Mya gasped as she witnessed the baby girl take three steps by herself before grabbing on to Don's fingers and burrowing her face into his shirt. Don propped Millie up for her return trip to Mya. Millie didn't hesitate and walked back to Mya. Don and Mya cheered while Emilia giggled over her accomplishment. Don felt Millie knew she was putting on a show and that she loved it. He wished that Valencia appreciated moments like this as much as Mya seemed to.

Little did he know that Valencia was just on the other side of the door.

Chapter 34

Mya lay on Don's right shoulder while talking softly and playing with his left hand. By then, Millie had been bathed, fed, and put to bed. Mya was still somewhat nervous. Although there was a lock on the door, she felt that Valencia would barge through it at any moment. Don could feel the tension in her body. She clung to him tighter than she had in their rendezvous. Don tried to calm her by talking to her about anything but Valencia.

"What does the name Emilia mean?" Don asked.

"Why do you assume that I know?" Mya asked.

"I think I know you well enough to know that you do know what Emilia means," Don said.

"Do you know or do you assume?" Mya asked.

"Just tell me."

Mya smiled. "You guessed right. I do know."

"It wasn't a guess."

"Whatever you say. Her name means rival."

"Rival. I wonder how that will play out if she lived up to the meaning of her name."

"Me too."

"Maybe she's your rival."

"In what way?"

"Well it's a given that I'm her favorite person in the world."

"Yes, but she was nice enough to allow me to share your attention tonight, so, I don't think it's me."

"True. So, what does your name mean?"

"The original spelling has an extra 'A' in it, but it means water."

"Water huh?" Don asked then laughed.

"Yes. Why are you laughing?" Mya asked.

"Is your name symbolic or something?"

"There is no sexual connotation associated with my name, mister."

"That's not why I'm laughing."

"Why are you laughing then?"

"Think about what you get when you put our three names in sequence staring with Emilia, yours, then mine."

Mya paused to think for a moment. She began to laugh too.

"Rival water lord," Mya said.

"Yeah. We sound like a family of angry pagans," Don said.

They laughed once more. Mya grew quiet and thought about what Don had just said. Mya keyed in on two words: "we" and "family". Then there was the joke about the names. Don proved to be a quick thinker. She liked that about him. He also had a level of depth that only came out when they were alone. There was something else he said that she wanted to know the answer to.

"So, what did you mean about my name being symbolic?" Mya asked.

"Because water is a necessity of life," Don said.

"Who would consider me a necessity of life?"

"I would."

Mya felt a wave of warmth radiate through her. Don gently squeezed Mya around her shoulder. Mya was starting to believe that Don was actually perfect. He seemed to know just what to say.

"Don," Mya said.

"I know, Mya. I love you," Don said.

Chapter 35

Friday, January 11, 2008

"Hey muscles. I need your help over here at Moore Hall on campus."

That was the text Mya sent to Don. Don called Mya to get her exact location. She was temporarily parked just south of the building attempting to haul a heavy tote full of clothes into an apartment on the first floor. Don was under the impression she was helping a friend move in.

That was until he took the tote inside.

"Surprise!" Mya called out.

"This is your room?" Don asked.

"What gave you the first clue?" Mya joked.

"I'm not sure. It was either the collage of pictures that include Millie and me or the purple and orange paisley design bedspread," Don said.

"You really do pay attention to detail."

"It's a gift and a curse at the same time. What made you do this?"

"Many reasons. It's about time I practice striking out on my own. I'm a tad further away from Parkland, but that's okay. But I have a place where you can visit me without having to run to a hotel."

"You can always visit me too."

"As much as I love my angry pagan family members, I am not fond of the thought of a scornful Latina in the same dwelling for any period of time."

Don laughed. "So, Millie and I are pagans now?"

"Without me, you're not. Why? Are you thinking of converting?" Mya asked playfully.

"What does Valencia mean?" Don asked.

"Brave. Why?" Mya answered.

"If I keep you both, they'll consider me a brave rival water lord." Don laughed.

"Not funny," Mya said as she lightly pushed him.

"Just kidding. I got something for you."

Don pulled out a gold necklace with a gold heart-shaped pendant on it.

"Turn around," Don said.

She did. Don reached over her head and fastened the necklace around her neck while she held her hair out of the way. Mya hurried over to the mirror hanging on the back of her door while uttering something high-pitched that Don couldn't understand.

"So…" Don said.

"I love it!" Mya said as she started to Don. She halted abruptly. Her eyes were fixed on the ring in Don's extended hand — a white gold band with ten small diamonds in it.

"Try it on," Don said softly.

Mya looked up at Don for a hint as to which hand she should put it on. Don offered no such notion. She chose the ring finger on her left hand. Mya jumped on Don and simultaneously threw her legs around his waist. Don caught her by her legs. Mya began feverishly kissing him. She broke off the kiss, hopped down, and ran to close the door.

"Get undressed," Mya said.

"What? You have a roommate," Don said.

"I know. That's why I closed the door. She's in her room," Mya said.

"Um, does she know I'm here?" Don asked.

"No." Mya walked up to Don and wrapped her arms around his waist.

"How is she going to react when she hears you making all sorts of noise?" Don asked.

"I'll be quiet."

"What do you know about this girl?"

"My dad's friend did a background check. She's docile."

"Docile? Is she a pet dog or something?"

"Well, she's here to keep me company when you and Millie aren't here. Besides, I'm allergic to cats. By that I mean I'm a dog person."

"Does that mean yes?"

"I don't know. Kinda."

"So, you've checked this apartment for hollow walls, trap doors, and peep holes, and hidden cameras?"

"You have a wild imagination. But yeah, I have."

Mya reached into Don's sweats to grab a hold of his dick.

"Don't say I didn't warn you," Don said.

Mya pulled out his dick over the waist of his sweats and boxers. She measured it in her hands. With both hands on it, there was still room enough for her to put a third hand on it.

Shit.

Mya had second thoughts.

"Meet me tonight," Mya said.

"Same place?" Don asked.

"Yeah."

"Make sure you get room nine-eighteen."

"Sure thing."

Don readjusted his pants and got ready to leave.

"Thank you for my ring, Don. It fits perfectly," Mya said.

"Size seven. It's a standard size. I'm glad you like it though. I love you, Mya," Don said.

"I love you, too, Don," Mya replied.

"Don't love me too. Just love me. That's good enough for me," Don said with a smile.

"Okay. I love you."

"I know. I love you. See you tonight."

Chapter 36

"Oh shit!" Mya screamed out.

Don froze in place.

"Okay, okay, okay. I'm ready. Try again," Mya said breathlessly.

Don tried again.

"Whew! Okay. Um…shit," Mya said. Don pulled out. He tried not to laugh, but he couldn't help it. She had been trying so hard for the past hour trying to adjust to his size, but to no avail. But, she wouldn't give up. She really wanted to have sex with Don.

"How much went in that time?" she asked proudly.

"Babe, we didn't get past the head," Don informed her.

"You sure?" Mya asked.

"Look. Your wet mark stops right here," Don said pointing to his dick.

"That's it? Damn. How big is that thing?"

"Big enough."

"We can try again. I'm ready."

"I got a better idea. How about we try something that will relax you?"

"Like what?"

"I like to refer to it as 'the biz'."

Don slid face first between her legs and began licking Mya's pussy. Instantly, Mya closed her eyes as her body submitted to the euphoria that stemmed from what was happening between her legs. She had never experienced this level of pleasure before. She could guess that a two-year age difference would mean that Don was a little more experienced than she was. She didn't want to think about him doing this with Valencia. It crossed her mind though. She also thought about how wet the bed would be the next morning and how glad she is that no one really recognizes her in public. It would be embarrassing to have a housekeeper of the hotel give the local news stations a story about how the daughter of Senator Brown has a crazy sex life. Her words.

Focus, Mya, she thought. *Just enjoy yourself.*

Mya felt her legs tremble. That was her warning sign. She tried to escape before it happened by propping herself up on the pillows. Don sensed it and dragged her to the edge of the bed. She shook even more. She looked to see his eyes. He looked away. She tried to reach for him, but her body was too weak to sit up. She crossed her ankles behind his back. She was about to cum. She let out a moan. Then another moan. Her whole body stiffened until she finally released.

"Mmm," Don said as he partook of her flowing juices.

Mya giggled. Her body was spent. She was satisfied and slightly embarrassed.

"I just blasted you in the face," she said.

"Mm hm," Don grunted.

"What are you doing down there?"

Don kissed her inner thigh. "Enjoying the view."

"Come up here and keep me warm."

"As you wish."

Don got up and lay on the bed next to her. Mya lay on top of him and kissed him. She then grabbed on to his dick and tried putting in her slippery pussy.

"Easy," Don said. "We'll get there eventually."

"I know."

"I didn't think you were a virgin."

"I'm not."

"I can't tell."

"Well every guy is not hung like you."

"I'm average."

Mya lifted his dick.

"In what world is this average?" Mya asked.

"In my world. I see it every day," Don said.

"You're used to it. That's why it seems normal to you."

Don laughed. Mya leaned over and kissed him on the lips. She then kissed him on the cheek and on the right side of his neck. He flinched. Mya lifted her head to look at his face. He was smiling.

"Are you ticklish?" Mya asked.

"No," Don answered.

"Then why did you flinch?"

"You weren't supposed to find that spot so soon."

"What spot?"

"I don't know what it is, but if you kiss me there it seemingly paralyzes me by sending a shock through my spine and I get really...turned on for some reason. You can't even breathe on it without me reacting."

"Really? Let's test this theory."

Mya slid off of Don to his right side. She made a mental note of the pool of fluid she left on Don's lower abdomen where she straddled him. She wanted to make that kind of puddle more often. She turned her attention to Don and tilted his head to the left. She gently licked his neck. His dick moved. Next, she kissed his neck and gave it a little suck. His dick moved again. Last, she got close enough to where Don could feel her breathe. His dick stood fully erect. Mya laughed.

"See what you've done?" Don asked jokingly.

"You weren't kidding, were you?" Mya replied.

"Not at all."

Mya made her way to the end of the bed and positioned herself between his legs.

"What are you doing?" Don asked.

Mya grabbed on to his dick and wet her lips. She looked up at Don and said, "Returning the favor."

Chapter 37

Tuesday, January 15, 2008

Don couldn't believe it. He had been fired from his job as an order management coordinator at Toys-R-Us. He was blindsided by the whole ordeal. Fortunately, he had a friend in Corporate that gave him the entire scoop.

Corporate had received a call a week earlier, alleging that Don had spanked his daughter at a local supermarket. The caller claimed to be a reporter and sought to get a representative to comment on the incident on the company's behalf.

The next day, a grainy video surfaced of a father striking a child of an indeterminate age. There were no discernable identifying features or marks on the man or child. The location was indeterminate as well. Yet the reporter threatened to go public with the information given to them from an unnamed source.

Corporate decided that they shouldn't take a chance with the video given that they manufacture and distribute products for children. They had no solid proof. Yet, they offered Don a severance package out of "good faith" that the incident wouldn't go public and pressured Don into signing a non-disclosure clause in reference to the details of his termination. His trusted friend in management told him that the alternative would not be in his best interests. The company was plotting to make him a scapegoat to save face by going public before the video had a chance to. They could honestly say that he doesn't work for them if he signed the documents before the reporter made good on the threat.

Don picked up Millie from his mother's house early that day. He told his mother the whole story. She suggested that he wait for things to settle down before he discussed any details with people that he trusted or associated with because the so-called reporter was likely someone he knew. He heeded the admonition and decided to be discreet. Don went to Parkland to inform Valencia about his misfortune.

"Oh no. Why they do that?" Valencia asked.

"The company is downsizing," Don lied.

"So, what we do now?" Valencia asked.

"We're fine. I'll find another job," Don said.

"Do you think we move to Florida now?"

"Why now?"

"I wanna be closer to my family."

"Here or there, you're still an ocean away."

"Not so much there though."

"Whatever. I never asked you to come here. My mother is here. That's why I'm here."

"I come with Millie. That why I come," Valencia said while playing with Millie's hand.

"I'm sure that's why you came. Look, I'm gonna go upstairs to see if Cathy has any ideas," Don said.

"You sure that why you go up there?"

"I don't have to explain nothing to you. If you don't like what I do, divorce me. All we have to do is get the papers and sign them."

Valencia frowned as if she was about to cry.

"Look. I'm out. I'm not about to watch you cry today," Don said then headed to the elevator with Emilia.

Once he stepped onto the fourth floor, Cathy noticed him immediately.

"Look! My babies have come to surprise me!" She announced.

Cathy approached, kissed Millie on the cheek, and said, "Baby number one and…" she kissed Don on the cheek, "baby number two."

"That's funny. I was born in eighty-four yet Emilia somehow surpassed me as baby number one," Don said sarcastically.

Cathy shook her head as she smiled. "You'll always be my baby. But you know when grandchildren are born, all the love is transferred to them."

"I'm learning that more and more each day," Don said.

"Oh, my poor baby. Now, what are you doing here in the middle of the day? Is it your day off?"

"You can say that. I go f-worded."

"Don't say that. She'll learn what that means one day."

"What? Fired?"

"Oh no."

"That's what Valencia said."

"Valencia…you know I only tolerate her because of you."

"When I hit the lottery, you can dispose of her any way you wish," Don said quietly.

"Hush. You're talking about the mother of my grandchild," Cathy said.

"I'm just saying what you were thinking. Accidents happen all the time."

Cathy laughed. "Medical professionals can be the most dangerous people in the world…if we chose to be."

"Oh, how I loathe your integrity."

Cathy laughed even harder. "Boy, you are all messed up in the head. Thank you for the laughs, though. What are you going to do now?"

"I have no plans, but I'll figure it out. I always do," Don said.

"That you do," Cathy agreed.

Cathy followed Don's eyes to figure out what caught his attention behind her. It was Mya. Brenda was pointing out something on a chart while Mya listened. Don noticed that she was wearing both the necklace and the ring.

"She's a sweet girl. A pretty girl too. But, she got herself a serious boyfriend, Don. So, if you're looking to replace the one downstairs, that one is off limits," Cathy explained.

"That's too bad," Don said. "I was just starting to like her."

Chapter 38

Wednesday, January 15, 2008

Don was wasted. He had reverted to being an introvert and went off the grid for the day. He turned off his phone and went walking the streets as soon as Valencia got to the apartment around 5:15. He felt he couldn't trust anyone in his inner circle. He wondered who would make such accusations against him.

It would be stupid for Valencia to do it because he made more money than she did and paid all the bills. It didn't make sense that Mya would do it. Cathy? No. Brenda? No. His mother? No. Rich? Maybe. What would Rich gain, though? He obviously wanted Valencia. The messages on her Facebook account were proof. Don never got to the bottom of that issue anyway. Valencia claimed Rich raped her but her English was so bad at times, it could mean anything.

It didn't make sense for Rich to try to ruin Don over Valencia, given that Don wanted nothing to do with her. Nevertheless, Rich wasn't in town. Maybe he didn't know the latest.

Don was stumbling out of the Barley House when he saw none other than Rich pulling up next to the sidewalk in his blue Chevy Impala.

"Man...what is your problem? You got three women calling me asking if I've heard from you," Rich said.

"Three?" Don asked.

"Yeah! Your mama, your wife, and Mya. Now why would Mya call me?" Rich inquired.

"Friends call friends," Don said.

"You must think I'm stupid."

"Yep."

"Get in, man. You're too drunk to walk and talk at the same time."

"I'm not."

"Man, get in. I'll take you home."

"Nope. Nope. Not there."

"Where you going? To your mama's house?"

"Nope," Don said as he landed in the passenger's seat.

"Oh...so you and Mya got something going on, huh? I knew it, I knew it! You still a dog, ain't ya?" Rich exclaimed.

"Nah."

"Mm hm. I'll ask Mya where she wants me to take you."

Mya gave Rich instructions on how to get to her apartment. Rich helped Don get into Mya's apartment and onto her bed. That's when Rich's phone rang. It was Valencia. Rich talked to her and assured her that Don was fine. Valencia wanted to hear from Don. Mya told Don not to tell Valencia where he was. Don nodded.

"Hello," Don answered.

"Don-Don, you okay?" Valencia asked.

"Yeah," Don said.

"You scare me," Valencia said.

"Oh," Don said.

"Where are you?" Valencia asked.

Don looked at Mya. Mya couldn't hear what Valencia was saying, but she gestured 'No' to Don.

"She told me not to tell you," Don said.

"What?" Valencia screamed.

Rich snatched his phone back and walked towards the bedroom door.

"Hello? You there?" Rich asked.

"Yes! What he saying?" Valencia asked.

Rich took one last glance back towards Mya and Don. Mya was shooing Rich out of the room and for a good reason. Mya was wearing a bathrobe, a small tee, and panties. After she let Don and Rich into the apartment, she got back in bed and pulled a blanket up to her waist. However, when Don made his stupid remark on the phone, Mya managed to slip off her panties and bury Don's face between her legs to keep him quiet. Don instinctively started licking Mya's pussy. She used the blanket to cover half of Don's body and up to her waist. Thus, she was trying to get rid of Rich.

Rich nearly missed the whole thing. He barely got a glimpse of Don's half covered body as he stepped outside the door and closed it.

"He's drunk, Valencia. I brought him over to a friend's surprise birthday party so I can keep an eye on him. That's why he said that because it's supposed to be a surprise," Rich explained.

"Oh okay. You bring him home?" Valencia asked.

"It's late and I've had a couple of drinks. I'll make sure he gets home first thing in the morning. Unless you need me to come check on you by myself," Rich said.

"Bye, Rich," Valencia said then hung up.

Rich knocked on Mya's door. She ignored him. Rich pressed his ear to the door. Mya sounded like she was enjoying what Don was doing to her. Rich was jealous.

"Open up little miss succubus. I gotta take him home," Rich said.

"Give me a second," Mya said. She counted ten more licks before she put on some pajama pants, tied the belt to her robe, and opened the door.

"I could have taken him home, you know?" Mya said.

"Yeah right. It's an emergency," Rich said as he pushed past Mya to help Don on his feet.

"What happened?" Mya asked.

"Why do you care?" Rich fired back.

"Because Don is my boyfriend. Whatever is important to him is important to me."

"Relax. It has nothing to do with Emilia. I'm just trying to play hero. That's all."

"I'm sure you are. If he wasn't so out of it, I'm pretty certain he'd kick your ass."

"Ha! Get real. You need to ask yourself why he's really messing around with you."

"What do you mean?"

"Ask him. You are not the first and trust me you will not be the last."

Chapter 39

Wednesday, January 16, 2008 — 8:46AM

Don was roused by the strong smell of coffee nearby. He noticed he was cold. He sat up and discovered he was completely naked and he wasn't in Millie's room — he was in the California king located in the master bedroom. Valencia was seated in a chair near the bed. She wasn't dressed for work. Don looked over at the clock to confirm what time it was. Then he looked back at Valencia. She was wearing a hoodie with the hood pulled over her head. Her hair was pulled to one side of her face. Don assumed she might be cold or had a cold until he realized she was wearing shorts.

Valencia set her coffee on the nightstand next to her and sat on the edge of the bed near Don.

"Hey," Valencia said.

"Where's Millie?" Don asked.

"She play in her crib. I give her toys," Valencia said.

"Why are you still here?" Don asked.

"I no work today. I need few days to get better."

"You sick?"

"No. You no remember?"

"No. Is that why I'm naked and in here?"

"Yes."

"So...what happened?"

Valencia removed the hood from her head and pulled her hair back. The right side of her face was swollen from her eye to her chin.

"What happened to you?" Don asked.

"You beat me, Don-Don," Valencia said and began to tear up.

"What? No!" Don said.

"You did," Valencia said.

"Why would I do that?"

"So you can forgive me. I ask you to. We even, no?"

Chapter 40

Monday, January 21, 2008

Valencia returned to work with only slight signs that she had bruising on her cheek, but the makeup she wore made it virtually impossible to tell anything had happened. Don had spent the last five days almost exclusively with Valencia. He tried to keep Mya at bay until he had the chance to explain what was going on. He had no memory of what actually happened. Only hazy glimpses that came and went, which he couldn't determine if they were actual occurrences or dreams.

Don's mother gave him the out he needed. Since Don wasn't working anymore, he kept Millie during the day. Thus, Don's mother was officially out of a babysitting job. However, on Friday, she demanded Don allow her grandchild to stay overnight. Don had spent most of the day indoors with Valencia in an attempt to appease her. Therefore, when his mother called for Emilia, Don capitalized on that opportunity. He told Valencia that he had to monitor his mother's health overnight and that he and Millie would return in the morning.

That Friday night, Don had Mya pick him up from his mother's house in case Valencia decided to drive over there to see if his car was there. He gave Mya an indication that something was going on that he couldn't explain but stopped short of telling Mya what allegedly happened to Valencia. He did tell Mya what happened at his job. She offered no opinions as to who might be responsible, but mentally filed the information as something she needed to look into.

Don spent the night with Mya. They tried having sex again. Mya was proud that she made a little more progress, which made Don laugh. It was the first time he had laughed in days. He didn't want to go back home. He felt safe with Mya. Don seemed to think more clearly when he was around Mya. He realized that Valencia said something that should have made him suspect her all along. She mentioned that they could move to Florida now that he was without a job.

Mya took Don back to his mother's house before sunrise at Don's request. He kissed Mya goodbye and watched Mya pout as he got out of the car. She was hoping to spend the weekend with Don. Instead, he spent the weekend with Valencia. Although he shared the same bed with Valencia that weekend, Don didn't have sex with her. He was merely there for damage control. His body may have been there with Valencia, but his heart and mind was with Mya. He planned to drop in on Mya the first chance he got.

Chapter 41

Tuesday, February 13, 2008

Donna Lane nearly refused to answer the phone when she saw that Valencia was the one calling her. Valencia had been calling the last few weeks to complain about how Donna's son, Adonis, was treating her.

Don returned to sleeping in Millie's room the very day Valencia went back to work. The next day, he brought Mya over to the apartment to play with Millie for a few hours before leaving with Mya for the night. He returned the following morning. However, when he brought Mya dinner at the hospital, he didn't attempt to stop by and talk to Valencia. Don hadn't attempted to hide his affair with Mya. Even Cathy knew about it.

Valencia refused to watch it go on any longer.

"Hello," Donna answered.

"Mizzez Lane. It's me. Valencia," Valencia said.

"I know, girl," Donna said. She could hear Millie crying loudly in the background. "What's wrong with Millie?"

"She with me," Valencia said.

"I know, but what's wrong with her?"

"I not do this anymore. He no love me."

"Who?"

"Don-Don."

"He's just hurt, Valencia. He's acting out. That's all."

"He love Millie, but no love me."

"Where are you? Is Millie at work with you?"

"No. She with me at home."

"Why is she crying?"

"Because I no let her go out the bathroom."

Donna became alarmed. "What are you doing?"

"I take Millie with me," Valencia said.

"Where are you going?" Donna asked.

Valencia started sobbing. Donna panicked. She sent Don a text while Valencia was still on the line.

"Val. Talk to me. Mama is here, but you have to talk to me," Donna said.

Valencia kept sobbing.

Come on, Adonis. Get there now! Donna thought.

Valencia eventually stopped crying. The phone went quiet for several moments. Donna couldn't even hear Emilia.

"Valencia? Valencia!" Donna shouted.

Suddenly, Emilia belted out a bloodcurdling shriek!

"Millie! Valencia, please answer me!" Donna called out.

Donna could hear a faint voice and a distant knocking.

It was Adonis. He was home now.

Chapter 42

Don spent the day making sure his arrangements for the following day were set in stone. Dinner reservations, tickets to the play, room nine-eighteen at the Highland, champagne, candy…the works. No flowers, though. He even stopped by Mya's apartment, while her roommate was there, to deliver a couple of oversized teddy bears. One for Mya that bore the embroidered message 'I love you!' The other for Renae that bore the embroidered message 'Obama loves you!' Renae was heavily into politics. She predicted that the nation would see a black president in her lifetime. She thought that the senator from Illinois had a legitimate shot. Don joked to Mya that Renae's passion for politics was the reason why she remained single.

Don had just stepped out of Mya's apartment when he received a text from his mother.

"Adonis! Drop what you're doing and go straight home!"

Naturally, the text alarmed him. He didn't bother calling his mother to find out what was going on. He had a clue.

"Shit! I forgot!" he said aloud to himself.

He had to watch Valencia on this day every year. She had attempted suicide on this day at least twice before Don had met her. At first, Don thought it had something to do with being alone; however, there was no reason for her to do it in 2007. She was seven months pregnant with Emilia and living with Don. He tried his best that year to make her feel loved and comfortable. He wasn't dating anyone else. He didn't do anything without her besides go to work. Don knew then that it was bigger than he first thought.

Don didn't attempt to lock the doors to his car. He ran up the stairs and unlocked the front door within seconds. As soon as he stepped inside, he heard Millie crying. Her cries were coming from the bathroom just outside her bedroom.

"Millie!" Don called out as he ran over to the bathroom door.

He knocked on the door and called out to Valencia and Millie. Millie crawled to the door and hit it. The door was locked. There was no sign of Valencia. Don lay flat on the floor to look under the door. He could see Millie's bare legs. There was something red on them. Don's eye caught a red streak that was smeared across the floor towards the bathtub. That's when he saw Valencia lying on the floor. She wasn't moving.

"Shhh…hold on Millie. Daddy's coming."

Don ran into the kitchen and grabbed a butter knife to pry open the door. He got it open and gently pushed it to prevent hurting Emilia.

"Come here, Millie…over here…Daddy needs to open the door."

Millie moved. Her crying subsided. Don peeked his head in to make sure he had room to open the door. He slipped inside and observed the scene as he picked up Emilia. Valencia's eyes were open. She blinked.

"I'll be right back, Valencia. Let me get Millie out of here. She doesn't need to see this," Don said.

He took Valencia's phone with him.

"Hello," Don said into the phone.

"Is Millie okay?" Donna asked frantically.

"She's fine," Don assured her.

"How's Valencia?" Donna asked.

"I don't know yet. She's alive."

"I'm on my way."

"Be safe, mama. Take your time. If you feel ill, pull over."

They ended the conversation. Don used a few baby wipes to clean Millie's face, arms, and legs. He checked her for any marks, cuts, and bruises. Nothing. Millie had simply crawled through her mother's blood. Don gave Millie a pacifier and placed her in her crib. He then hurried into the bathroom to assess the situation.

"I no hurt your daughter," Valencia said candidly.

Don kneeled next to Valencia. "But, you hurt my daughter's mother."

"Why you care?" Valencia asked.

"Because it will make Millie sad to know that you're gone," Don said.

"That all you care for. Millie. You no care."

"Val. I care. Where are you hurt? Tell me."

"Show me you care."

Valencia was on her right side in the fetal position right in front of the toilet, with her head near the bathtub and her legs towards the door. Don didn't want to move her until he could locate the source of the bleeding. He couldn't see any sharp objects. She wasn't awkwardly leaning as if one was piercing her from underneath. In the past, she had used sewing needles to cut her wrist. But, there was way more blood in this instance.

Valencia was wearing a t-shirt. She was naked from the waist down. That's when Don noticed a trickle of blood by her ankles. He leaned over her to get a better look.

"Val...no," Don said.

What he saw disturbed him. He gently lifted Valencia's left leg straight up. Valencia had inserted a steak knife (handle-first) into her vagina, all the way to the base of the blade. She also inserted another one the same way into her rectum. No parts of the blades were cutting her internally. Don was grateful for that. The blades did cut the back of her legs and the inside of her thigh when she folded her legs. Don removed both of them, sat her up, and helped her to her feet. He had her sit on the toilet so he could examine her further.

He noticed a new gash on her left wrist. It was trying to clot for the most part. Don assumed she used one of the steak knives because the wound was thin and rigid.

Don pulled out a clean towel and a first aid kit that contained gauze and bandages. Valencia watched as he cleaned and dressed it. There was much care in how he did it. Valencia noticed that. Don took off her shirt to make sure she wasn't hurt anywhere else. Nothing. He checked her head, hair, eyes, and ears.

"Say ah," Don said.

"Ah," Valencia said without opening her mouth.

"No, silly. Open your mouth and say it," Don said with a smile.

She did. She didn't realize he was checking for small sharp objects such as razor blades and sewing needles. Don kneeled in front of her.

"Did you eat today?" Don asked.

"No," Valencia answered.

"Drink anything?" Don asked.

"Some juice," Valencia said.

"What kind?"

"Orange juice."

"With pulp?"

Valencia nodded. Don placed his hands on Valencia's thighs.

"Anything else?" Don asked.

"No," Valencia answered.

"No medications or anything?"

"No."

"Okay. How are you feeling health-wise? Are you dizzy or anything?"

"No."

"Okay…How did I do?"

Valencia gave a quick weak smile then looked down. She then grabbed him by his face and kissed him desperately. Don felt an urge to reject it, but he realized it was better not to. It was okay for now. He was saving a life.

Chapter 43

Donna Lane arrived shortly after Don convinced Valencia to shower while he stayed in the bathroom with her. He wanted to keep an eye on her at all times. Once she was dressed, Don entrusted Val into his mother's care until he finished cleaning up the mess in the bathroom. Donna had already found Millie and was hugging her snugly on the couch. When Valencia sat down next to her, Donna put her arm around Val and held her close.

"My girls," Donna said.

That evening, Don insisted on following Donna home to make sure she made it safely. He had Valencia and Emilia in the car with him. Don walked his mother to the door. Donna had held her tongue to prevent from taking sides, but now, she had a message for Don.

"Adonis, that is your wife. God is gonna hold you accountable if you don't look after her like you should," Donna said.

"This isn't my fault," Don said.

"It may not be completely your fault. But, I know when my son has a hand in something. You know that she wants your love and approval. And I know that you're good at withholding love and building walls. You can starve a person emotionally. And that's not always a good thing," Donna explained.

"You don't know her, though, Mama," Don said.

"What has she done to you lately?"

"Nothing I can prove."

"If God held everything you've done in the past against you, where would you be?"

"Nowhere good."

"Exactly. Adonis, you need to reconcile. She's obviously broken now. Everything will be fine from now on. You'll see. Do know that God will not bless you if you continue to live a double life."

"We'll see."

"Promise you'll try," Donna requested.

"I will," Don said.

Don didn't intend to try that night. He spent the night in Millie's room.

Chapter 44

Don was roused by a soft but repetitive tapping noise. He realized it was coming from the door. He hopped out of bed before the noise could wake Millie. He opened the door. Of course, it was Valencia. She was wearing only a black bra and panties. Don could tell by the way her bra straps were hanging that she had lost weight.

Val had been starving herself with the hope that Don would forgive her and leave Mya alone. Don responded by shunning her even more and keeping Millie away from her for days at a time. He didn't want Millie to see her mother wasting away. He pretended not to notice it himself, but he refused to play her deadly game.

Valencia instantly started to cry at the sight of him. Don sighed heavily, partially concealing himself with the door.

"What do you want?" Don asked quietly.

"Why...you...no...touch me?" Val asked through a river of tears and between breaths. She was hyperventilating.

"Shh…" Don said as he stepped through the door to console Valencia. He shut Millie's door behind him and scooped up Valencia in one fell swoop. Valencia quickly wrapped her legs and arms around Don, but she really didn't need to. He easily managed her new weight with one arm. He carried her to the room they once shared while Valencia buried her face in his neck. She missed his scent. His touch. She wasn't sure what Don was going to do, but she took advantage of the physical contact he offered for the moment.

Don closed the door behind him with his free hand a lowered Valencia onto her back. Valencia was reluctant to release her hold, but, since Don was halfway on the bed with her, she figured she had time to convince him to stay before he made it to the door. However, Don lay next to her on his left side, propped up on his left elbow so he could look her in the eye. Valencia became overwhelmed with the unexpected duration of his presence.

"Talk to me," Don said. "Why are you doing this to yourself?"

"You no love me no more," Valencia said.

"That's not true. I'll always have love for you because you gave me Millie. But, I don't like how you treat our marriage. It's a joke to you," Don said.

"No yoke," Valencia said.

"Well whatever you call it, I don't like what you do. It's not okay with me. But, no matter how I respond, it's not okay to stop eating. I don't want Millie to watch you starve yourself."

"No, no. I eat."

"You will?"

"Jes, I eat." Valencia gently grabbed his right arm and draped it over her body. Don ran his hand up her spine. Her exposed bones told Don just how much Valencia emaciated herself.

"I don't believe you," Don said.

Valencia grew desperate. "I eat! Prometo. I eat. I eat, I be nice to Millie, I chain my number. I promise. Just touch me, Don-Don."

She pulled Don with all she had to encourage him to get on top of her. Their faces were nearly touching.

"Kiss me, Don-Don. Touch me. I promise I eat," Valencia said.

Don gave her a quick peck on the lips.

"You promise?" Don asked.

Valencia used Don's right hand to help her remove her panties. Don pulled them the rest of the way when she could no longer reach.

"I promise, Don-Don. Just fuck me, please," Valencia whispered.

Don gave in. He remembered a time when he wasn't reluctant to give Valencia what she wanted. Valencia reached into his shorts and pulled out his dick. Don managed to take of his shorts and boxers while remaining engaged in a lengthy kiss with Valencia. She guided his dick into her pussy and stretched her legs outward to accept more of Don. The fit was glove-like; as if their counterparts were made for one another.

"Don-Don...promise me," Valencia whispered.

"Promise what?" Don asked between breaths.

"Promise...no more...no more silly girl," Valencia said.

Don stopped thrusting and looked Valencia in the face.

"What are you offering me?" Don asked.

Valencia knew without a doubt the one thing that would make Don consider cutting ties with Mya. She looked at him confidently and said,

"A baby boy."

"When?" Don asked. The offer was provocative, so he bit.

"We start right now. Give him to me, Don-Don."

Chapter 45

Wednesday, February 14, 2008 — 7:14AM

Don slipped out of bed and left Valencia behind to send Mya a text and check his phone for messages. He and Mya made a bet. The first person to text the other a Valentine's message got to have their way in bed that night. Don had planned on having Mya lay on her side in front of him as he ever so gently pounded her from behind. Mya was better at taking dick when she couldn't look down and see it. And since it was Valentine's Day, Don considered it slightly more romantic than doggy style or bending her over a couch and thrashing her.

Yeah…slightly.

His phone was in Millie's room. Don managed to get to his phone without waking Millie. He left the door partially open because the door would creak when it closed. Besides, he wouldn't stay long. He had to get back in bed before Valencia noticed he was gone.

"Happy V-day."

That was the message Don sent to Mya.

"I so beat you!" Mya texted back.

"Yeah, I know. Midnight texts are unfair." Don replied. Mya texted him right at midnight. He would have received it had he not been preoccupied with Valencia.

"Well then, I'll try to be fair tonight and choose things we can both enjoy." Mya texted.

"How so?"

"Well, I plan for you to go all in again tonight. You enjoy that, don't you?"

Don never actually fit all the way in like he did with Valencia. He just told Mya that to protect her feelings. She was so excited about accomplishing it, but Don knew that if she didn't slow down, his size would actually hurt her.

"All the way sounds good." Don texted in reply.

He actually won in a way. The only time he told Mya that he put his dick all the way in her pussy was when they had sex laying on their sides. Their sexual desires were in sync, although they didn't realize it. Mya enjoyed when Don fucked her from behind. Her words. She never verbally told Don that though.

"Good. I can't wait to see you tonight." Mya texted.

"Well, I tend to have that effect on women." Don texted back.

"Really? You had to take it there."

"Okay, okay. I can't wait to see you."

"Was that so hard? LOL"

"Not at all."

"I gotta get my day started. Ttyl. I love you." Mya texted.

"I love you." Don replied.

Don put away his phone and made it to the door. As soon as he opened it, he saw Valencia standing there; right in front of the door.

"Did you tell her?" Valencia asked.

Don thought about lying about what he was doing, but he figured that she witnessed him texting on his phone.

"Yes. I told her I'd explain later in person," Don said.

"Why?" Valencia asked.

"I owe her that much," Don said.

"She tell you she love you?"

"No, but I know she really likes me a lot."

"Why you care?"

"She's a good person, Val. She did nothing wrong. It's not her fault. Okay?"

"Okay." Valencia knew if she pushed him too hard, he could easily go back on what he promised. However, Don never actually promised to never see Mya again. Valencia took the intimacy as him agreeing to what she requested. Further, his texting Mya that their fling was over was definitely a step in Valencia's favor. Her words.

"Shower with me," Valencia demanded in a passive voice.

"You're trying to have sex with me, aren't you?" Don asked.

Valencia wore a sly smile. "Maybe."

"I know that's your plan. You better eat today. Come on. Let's shower before Millie wakes up."

Chapter 46

Don did intend on telling Mya something that day. He just didn't know what to say or how to say it. When to say it was proving to be just as difficult. Both Mya and Valencia were at Parkland. Given that Valencia worked on the first floor, she would likely see Don enter the building or leaving.

No matter how non-confrontational Mya and Valencia seemed to be, Don didn't trust that Valencia wouldn't approach Mya about the basis of what he and Mya talked about. Which would likely cause Mya's inner Lakeisha to come out and give a tell-all about what he and Mya have been doing and for how long. Which would cause Valencia to get so upset that she'd start talking so fast that she no longer makes sense in any language and Mya and Valencia would start fighting.

His thoughts.

Instead, Don took the indirect approach.

Don cashed in a huge favor with Cathy. He had more than enough leverage to do so with Millie alone. Don took advantage of the fact that

Cathy really wanted to babysit Millie and convinced her to take the day off so she could. As long as she promised not to do anything work-related, Don agreed to let Millie stay with Cathy overnight. Don wasn't worried about Cathy multi-tasking and forgetting about Millie, he just wanted Cathy to enjoy her time with Millie. He then talked Cathy into allowing Mya to leave at noon and make up her hours on the weekend. Cathy already knew that he was pursuing Mya and that he was her secret boyfriend, so she agreed to that without reservation. She wanted a grandson, but not from Valencia. If Don thought that Mya was worth dating then Cathy supported the relationship fully.

Mya was surprised when she was told to leave for the day at noon. Now that she was off, Mya wanted to meet up with Don for a few hours. Don said that he would meet her at her apartment, but when she arrived, a limousine with a chauffeur was there to usher her to her next destination. When she got inside the limo, there was a card on the seat. It was plain but there was a message on it:

I'm waiting…

-Don

Mya laughed and smiled big. Her boyfriend was a few steps ahead of her. Don arranged for Mya to spend a couple of hours at Pure Spa and Salon for some relaxation and a touch up on her hair. Mya's next destination was Chanel. There, she was fitted for an evening gown, shoes, and the jewelry to match. Mya couldn't take any more surprises. She was ready to see Don. The chauffeur assured Mya that she would meet him at the next stop.

The limo arrived at the AT&T Performance Arts Center nearly ten minutes later than expected, but Don didn't fret because they were still early. Mya didn't recognize Don at first. She thought he was another stranger opening the limo door for her. She hadn't seen him in a tuxedo before.

"You look even better than I imagined you would," Don said.

"Thank you, Don. What's all this?" Mya asked.

"A play," Don said.

"No silly. This limo, the spa…everything has been amazing thus far," Mya said.

"Oh that? I thought you might enjoy a little time to yourself."

"True. But the whole time I was wondering when I was going to see you."

"Here I am."

"I can see that. So, what are we here to see?"

"A play about a distant relative of mine."

"Really? Who?" Mya asked.

"Don Quixote," Don said.

Mya laughed. "What? No *Romeo and Juliet*?"

"*Romeo and Juliet* ended this past weekend," a tall man with light skin wearing a fancy tuxedo said from behind Don. Don turned and noticed the man was being closely followed by two men; obvious bodyguards.

"Hi, Daddy. What are you doing here?" Mya said.

Daddy? Don thought.

"Same thing as you apparently. You look *just wonderful*, darling. Who is your friend?" Mr. Brown asked referring to Don as he positioned himself halfway between the two of them.

"Daddy, I want you to meet—"

"Don Lane," Don interjected while extending his hand.

"Lane…Have we met before?" Mr. Brown asked.

"I'm not sure I even got your name, sir," Don said.

Mr. Brown laughed. "Oh, I'm sorry. I just assumed that my daughter here told you about me. I'm Senator Jamerson Brown."

Don was stunned but managed the shock.

"Well, Senator, I have no reason to believe that our paths have crossed," Don said.

"You sure?" Senator Brown asked.

"Daddy, you're not being polite," Mya said. Mya knew that her father was implying that Don might have a criminal history. Her father was a police officer before he started dabbling into politics.

"What'd I do?" Senator Brown asked as if he were wrongly accused. "Where are your seats? I can have Franks escort you to prevent you from being held up."

Don pulled the tickets from the inner pocket of his jacket.

"Row F. Center section," Don said proudly.

"Beautiful! Not too close, not too far. You know, your mother and I will be seated right behind you," Senator Brown said to Mya. "Your mother is already seated. I can take you to your seats myself."

The idea didn't sit well with Mya. She looked over at Don then back at her father.

"You know what, Daddy? I didn't intend for anyone but my date to escort me to my seat," Mya said.

Senator Brown gave a weak smile, looked over at Don, then back at Mya.

"You two have fun," he said.

"Thank you, Daddy," Mya said.

Senator Brown walked into the building. Don waved briefly.

Mya stepped closer to Don and said,

"He won't let us be. Give me the tickets."

Chapter 47

Mya ended up giving the tickets to a random couple. Mya and Don then took a limo ride around the city and talked just to kill time until their scheduled dinner reservation at Olivella's. Mya loved that place.

After dinner, the couple made it to room nine-eighteen. Mya was pleased with the accommodations, the planning, and the detail. But, she was concerned about something. She noticed that Don's countenance had declined gradually since they ran into her father. Mya didn't know what was going through his mind, but she wanted to make sure Don heard her point of view.

"Are you mad at me?" Mya asked.

"What? Why would I be mad at you?" Don inquired.

"It's just that…I was going to tell you, but I didn't know how," Mya said.

"Wait a minute. First of all, I have no clue what you're talking about. Second, I have no clue where this is coming from. I thought we were having a great time," Don replied.

"Well I thought you were upset about me not telling you about my dad."

"About him being a senator?"

"Yes."

"Well, that was a shock, but that's not a deal breaker."

"It's not?"

"No. I actually think it's kinda hot that my girlfriend has bodyguards around every corner," Don said smiling. He leaned in close and gave Mya a quick peck on the lips.

"Then why are you upset with me?" Mya asked.

"What makes you think I'm upset?"

"You've been somewhat off. It's hard to explain how. But, you never miss the opportunity to say something witty or at least acknowledge that you notice the odd things people around us say or do. Tonight? Nothing."

"And that means I'm upset? Distracted, maybe. But not upset."

"Then there's the drinking."

"Special occasion?"

"Not even close. Champagne in the limo, tequila at dinner, and three glasses of champagne since we've walked in."

"And that means..."

"You never have more than one drink unless you're upset about something. And this time I know it's me because you haven't attempted to get me out of this dress yet."

Don put down his glass and sighed heavily. He lay back on the bed and stared at the ceiling in silence. Mya observed from the middle of the bed. She inched closer to him and crisscrossed her legs at his right side. She was about to say something to him until she noticed a single tear spill from his right eye. Mya immediately lay next to Don. She would have missed the tear had she not been waiting for him to answer. His demeanor didn't change. He didn't frown. Didn't make a sound.

Mya was worried. She couldn't help but feel it was somehow her fault. She wasn't sure if touching him was a good or bad idea, but she did it anyway.

"Donnie…please. Just talk to me. You can tell me anything," Mya said.

Don didn't respond. Mya definitely felt it had something to do with her.

"Donnie. Look at me…Can you look at me, please? Can I see your pretty eyes? One time…for me?" Mya pleaded.

Don looked at her.

"Thank you. Can you tell me what's wrong?" Mya asked.

"I can't do it anymore," Don said.

Chapter 48

Valencia was ecstatic to see Don walk into the bedroom just before ten that night. She assumed that Don was likely there to make the most of the time they had alone. Millie was to be with Cathy until the morning. Valencia sat up in bed hoping that Don noticed that she was awake. He headed straight for the closet. Valencia hopped out of bed and walked to the doorway of the closet.

"Hey handsome," Valencia said.

Don was changing out of the tux. Don didn't look in her direction, but he answered in a cordial manner.

"Hey. What are you doing up?" Don asked.

"I wait for my honey," Valencia said.

"Is that so? I better leave before he gets here," Don said with a smile.

Too soon for a joke like that? Don thought to himself while trying to oversell his smile.

"Hey..."

"Just kidding."

"You better be. So, how go your work interviews?"

Don had to give Valencia a reason for wearing a tux. An early funeral and a few job interviews. It made sense to Valencia.

"Pretty good. I'm not sure they will call me, though. I'm not exactly what they are looking for. Did you eat today?"

"Jes. I eat fish for dinner," Valencia reported.

"Good," Don said.

"Did you eat?"

"Of course."

"With that girl?"

Don't lie, Don thought.

"Yes," Don said.

"Do you tell her?" Valencia asked.

"Yes."

"How did she take it?"

Don thought about it before he spoke.

Mya had asked him what he meant when he said couldn't do it anymore. That's when he explained that he felt trapped into being with Valencia. He tried to leave, but she pulled the elaborate suicide attempt that kept him in check. He didn't like feeling as if he had to walk on eggshells around Valencia for fear she might do something to Millie. Or herself. Or both Millie and herself. What's worse than that was the fact that his own mother blamed him as if he was the cause. Donna seemingly sided with Valencia despite her indiscretions.

Mentally spent, Don felt that was the last straw. Unfortunately, Don was confused about how to handle his relationship with Mya going forward.

Don didn't hide the fact that he slept with Valencia. He explained the feeling of doing the something to save the mother of his child versus remaining faithful to the woman he claims has his heart. He said that he made the decision for Millie and that it was a temporary fix until he could find a permanent solution.

Mya took the news in stride and even suggested that she take a lesser role in his life until he figured it out. Don thought she meant friends, but Mya explained that instead of being open about their relationship, she would keep their relationship a secret. She then suggested that he go home and check on Valencia.

Mya was hurt and it would be years before she ever truly forgave him. Her Mr. Perfect turned out to be a mere mortal after all, but he was still lovable.

Don told none of this to Valencia.

"She'll be okay. I doubt if she will ever talk to me again. I broke her…trust," Don said.

"Oh. You still have me, no?" Valencia asked.

"Yeah I do. Hey look. I'm gonna go for a few drinks. You good here?"

"Jes. Drink for me too."

"Will do. No drinks for you anytime soon."

"Nope. We want a baby!"

Don arrived back at room nine-eighteen at about 10:15. Mya met Don at the door. She hugged Don as if he safely returned from an overseas tour of duty.

"What's this all about?" Don asked.

"I didn't think you would be able to get away tonight," Mya said.

"No stunts tonight. We're all good," Don said.

"How good?" Mya asked.

"You and me or me and her?"

"You and her."

"We'll never be good anymore."

"Do you love her?"

"Am I in love with her or do I have love for her?"

"Both."

"What's wrong, Mya?"

"I need to know."

Don looked at Mya and offered a reassuring smile. Don knew she didn't care about him loving Valencia. There was something else.

"Mya, I'm not going anywhere. Okay?" Don said.

"Prove it," Mya said then smiled.

"I'm here."

"Not good enough."

"What would you suggest as an act of proof?"

"Well...you can always do that thing I like."

"What thing?"

"You know."

"Say it," Don said.

"I want you to do...what you do with your tongue," Mya said sheepishly.

"Talk?" Don was playing dumb.

"No," Mya said in a whiny tone.

"Then what?"

"You know. Down there."

"Tell me."

"I want...I want you to...give me the biz."

Don laughed. "Now was that so hard?"

"Yes!" Mya said with an embarrassed smile.

"Well, this will be an easy test. The question is...will this satisfy your doubts?"

"For now...That is, until the next time I need a fix."

Chapter 49

Wednesday, March 26, 2008

It had been two years since Diana Vargas passed away. Don had never thought of her more before that day. Valencia revealed to Don that she was pregnant that morning. And, according to her superstitions, her swollen breasts and other symptoms indicated that she was having a boy. Don was more skeptical and thought that her assumptions were premature.

Part of him wanted to believe her. A parent can never replace a child with another one. Another child, though, would offer a measure of consolation. However, for Don, the pregnancy added stress to an already stressful juggling act. Millie obviously at the center.

Millie's well-being came first. Then there was Mya — the obvious choice — on one side. Emilia seemed to be a fan of Mya. Last, there was Valencia. Besides having one on the way, she was Emilia's mother. And Don's wife. With those factors in mind, Don had to handle Valencia more delicately and at least make her believe she was just as important to him as Millie was. But, what about Mya?

Don and Cathy met at a memorial for Diana and baby Dejahmi at the intersection where the wreck occurred. Diana's father insisted that she and her baby be laid to rest in Philly, so Cathy convinced a non-profit organization, called MADD (Mothers Against Drunk Driving), to erect a memorial in their honor. After leaving the memorial, Cathy went back home to grieve alone. Don, on the other hand, went inside Parkland.

Don found Mya standing at the nurses' station. He discreetly tapped her on the butt as he walked past and stepped into an empty room. She followed closely behind and Don closed the door as soon as she entered the room. The act, although noticed by few, evoked catcalls from the nurses' station. Mya didn't hesitate to throw her arms around Don's neck and begin kissing him. Don went with it for a moment before gently prying her arms off him in an effort to stop her.

"Wait. I can't," Don said.

"Why not?" Mya asked concerned.

"I came here to tell you something and all you're doing is making me change my mind about saying it," Don reported.

"Well, from the way you said that, I would say that's a good thing," Mya said.

"Maybe."

"So. What up?" Mya folded her arms. That was her defensive stance that she used to brace herself for something she was unprepared for.

"She's pregnant."

"Valencia?" Mya dropped her hands to her side.

"Yes," Don said.

"How pregnant?"

"I don't know. I assume about six weeks."

"You assume? Is she showing at all?"

"Yeah," Don said as he held his hand a couple of inches from Mya's stomach. "About that much."

"With her history, are you sure that the baby is yours?"

To his surprise, those words stung Don. He was offended on Valencia's behalf. It was a reality that he hadn't taken into account. He never asked. He wasn't sure how far along Valencia was before she began showing with Emilia. Valencia's sudden urge to have a baby came out of nowhere. He thought it was onset by her jealousy, but now he realized that it could be a guise to cover up the fact that she was already pregnant.

"No. I guess I don't know if the baby is mine," Don said.

"So, what are you going to do?" Mya asked.

"What do you mean? I don't believe in abortion!"

"No, no, no. I'm sorry. I-I wasn't suggesting that. It came out wrong."

"Look, the reason why I came here is to tell you. Now that you know, you have a decision to make."

Mya fought back tears to appear brave.

"I don't know, Don," Mya said.

Don paused before answering, and then said, "If you even have to think about it, then it's not worth it."

He left.

Mya was too stunned to follow. She didn't cry immediately, but she wanted to. Anger took over first. She hated him for the moment. He chose a whore and her unborn child over Mya. Her words.

That's strike two, Don.

Chapter 50

Friday, April 25, 2008

By the time Millie turned one, Don started to question just how pregnant Valencia was. Valencia would wear a hoodie and shorts around the apartment, claiming she was cold all the time. One thing that proved true was her appetite. Don noticed that she a pudge forming around her waistline. In March, she would let him rub her stomach as he made comments about their baby on the way. But by mid-April, Don began to see there was no growth. No tightening. No change at all.

That's when he found it. A few days before Valencia's birthday, Don discovered a used tampon floating in the toilet. Don waited until Millie's birthday to confront Valencia.

Once Millie was sound asleep, Don questioned Valencia about the pregnancy. She was in bed waiting for Don to return from Millie's room.

"There you are," Valencia said.

"Here I am," Don said.

"Come here. We wait for you," Valencia said.

"We? You speak French now?" Don asked sarcastically.

"No silly. Me and—"

"The mouse in your pocket?"

"Why so mean?"

"Why did you lie to me?"

"I no understand. I no lie."

"Valencia. I wasn't always a jobless bum. I went to nursing school. I know that bleeding is rare with pregnancy, but it does happen. However, a full-blown period is an indication of something else," Don explained.

Valencia stared in disbelief.

"When were you going to tell me?" Don asked.

"I—" Valencia started.

"You, being over two months pregnant, could make a pee stick light up positive in seconds. Care to pee on one?"

"Okay, okay. I no lie anymore."

"You know what?...Never mind. Forget it."

Don stood to leave.

"Wait! We try again! I promise I get pregnant this time," Valencia said.

"No thanks. I'm glad you're not pregnant. I don't need a baby right now anyway," Don said.

He left the room. Instead of stepping into Emilia's room, he decided to text Mya. It was about 8:15.

"Hey. Any plans?" Don texted.

"Nothing solid. What's up?" Mya texted back.

"I'm coming over." Don texted.

"When?" Mya replied.

"Now."

Chapter 51

Tuesday, June 17, 2008

Mya watched every game of the NBA Finals with Don. Don's defending champion Spurs didn't make it, so he was rooting against Kobe Bryant and the Lakers. Boston posed no threat to Don's hope for Tim Duncan to retire as the next great behind Jordan. Thus, he was elated when the Celtics ended the series that night. Mya was a Dallas, Lebron, and Kobe fan, but she kept her competitive spirit in check while her boyfriend celebrated each win.

Mya celebrated the fact that Valencia was no longer pregnant. Don allowed Mya to believe that Valencia had a miscarriage. If he told Mya the truth, she might have confronted Valencia for lying or ridiculed Don for running away with the idea. His words. It seemed that Don would do anything to save face.

Mya noticed that Don seemed a bit distant, but she assumed he was either grieving the loss of another child (a feeling she didn't understand) or he was holding a grudge against her for not being more decisive when it came to their relationship. She would have stayed with Don until the baby was proven to be his. And even if the baby was Don's, she likely would have stuck with him. Besides, he hadn't completely struck out with her yet. Given that there was no longer a baby, Mya gave Don the benefit of the doubt. He was back down to one strike. Well, one and a half. Her words.

At the conclusion of the NBA Finals, Mya gave Don a congratulatory kiss, hoping to initiate a sexual encounter. She would even settle for a quickie. She was in forbidden territory — Don's apartment. Valencia was at work. Being the girl on the side in a situation like that made Mya feel like a bad girl. And that feeling aroused Mya at that very moment.

Don hugged and kissed her back. He grabbed a handful of Mya's ass — clothed in tight jeans — and squeezed. She was further excited by that and grabbed Don by his dick.

"That's all you want, huh?" Don asked.

"No. I want you. This is definitely a big plus though," Mya said as she jiggled his dick.

"I'm sure," Don replied.

"It is. What? You think I can't go without it?" Mya asked.

She searched for a clue in Don's eyes as to how he felt.

Don grabbed Mya's left hand with his right. "I bet you don't even wear this when I'm not around," Don said referring to the ring.

"Are you crazy? I wear this every day."

"Not around your family."

Mya gave a telling glare. She realized that Don must have noticed that she concealed her hand when they ran into Mya's father on Valentine's Day.

"It's too soon," Mya said.

"It wasn't too soon when I gave it to you," Don said.

"No but—"

"You don't love me. Give me my ring back," Don said as he removed it from her finger.

"No," Mya protested without pulling back her hand.

Don slipped the ring onto his pinky using only his right hand.

"You don't want this," Don said. He pulled her closer to him by her ass by putting his hands in her back pockets.

Mya was hoping Don was kidding, but she couldn't tell. She kissed him.

"Yes I do. It's my ring," Mya said.

"Are you going to wear it around your family?" Don asked.

"That's not fair."

"Wrong answer."

"Donnie!"

"You gotta go. Val will be home any minute."

"Okay. Can I have my ring back?"

"I'll think about it. Go."

Don gave her a quick kiss.

Mya left.

Mya spent the entire short drive back to her apartment glancing at her left hand. She felt naked without her ring. As soon as she stepped into her apartment, she sent Don a text.

"Mad at you."

"For what?" Don texted back.

"I want my ring back!" Mya texted.

"You have it. Check your back pocket." Don replied.

Excited, Mya reached into her back pocket. She then checked the other.

"There's no ring in my back pocket funny man. Give it back." Mya texted.

"Not kidding. I gave it back to you. Check again." Don replied.

Sudden dread overcame Mya. She checked each corner of her pockets. Even her front pockets. She rechecked her back pockets a third time and discovered a hole. Mya texted Don again.

"Seriously Don. I don't have it!"

"You better because neither do I." Don texted back.

Mya panicked. She ran outside to check her car, the parking lot, the small patch of grass near her apartment building. She checked her apartment from the door to her room. All to no avail. She felt like crap. Don's next text didn't make her feel any better.

"I knew you didn't care about me. You should have just gave it back to me."

Chapter 52

Sunday, June 22, 2008

Valencia wasn't expecting Don that day.

Although he was cordial to her, the news of her faked pregnancy took its toll on their already-fragile relationship. She knew she couldn't keep the charade going for too long. She was trying to buy herself some time until she actually got pregnant. Don, though, didn't show much interest in having sex with Valencia. At first, she thought if she told him she was pregnant, Don would have sex with her more often because they would have a renewed bond. That didn't work. Valencia then resorted to having sex with Don in his sleep. Sometimes he would let her. Other times, he would wake up and go to Millie's room. In any case, she couldn't quite time it right and she didn't get pregnant.

Don was good at avoiding Valencia on days that had only significance to her. She was used to it by now. And even if he did make an appearance, it had nothing to do with what that day represented. Valencia reacted accordingly when Don showed up at Parkland.

"Hey, Don-Don. What are you doing here?" Valencia asked.

"I'm looking for you," Don said.

"For me? Por que?" Valencia asked.

"I came to ask why you don't wear your ring," Don said.

"It's too big."

"Okay. Where is it?"

"At home."

"Are you sure?"

Valencia got nervous. She'd been looking for it since she returned from Buenos Aires, but she had never located it.

"I think I left it in Argentina," Valencia admitted.

"Really? That's amazing," Don said as he pulled his hands out his pockets. On his left pinky was Valencia's ring — a white gold band with ten diamonds in it.

When Don was cleaning out the apartment in January, he raided Valencia's jewelry box to confiscate all the jewelry he purchased for her. He noticed she left her wedding band behind. She claimed she didn't wear it because it was too big, which was true. Nevertheless, even after six months of marriage, she hadn't attempted to get it sized. Don figured it meant nothing to her. To Don, it represented a commitment. So, he took the ring along with the gold necklace with a heart-shaped pendant on it that he bought for her on Valentine's Day in 2006. The rest of the jewelry he purchased for her was not in there. Mostly diamonds, she must have taken them with her.

"You find it?" Valencia asked.

"Oh this? Try it on," Don said as he handed her the ring.

The ring fit perfectly.

"It fit! How?" Valencia asked.

Tr3.6.6

"I had it sized for your narrow finger."

"Aw, thank you baby! I worry so much when I no find."

She leaned over the counter and kissed him.

Don only pretended to stuff the ring in Mya's back pocket. It was dumb luck that the pocket had a hole in it. Mya felt like a villain while Don got to play hero to his wife.

"You're welcome, Val. Happy anniversary," Don said.

"Happy anniversary, Don-Don!" Valencia said.

Chapter 53

Tuesday, November 18, 2008 — 12:00AM

Don stayed awake to be the first to acknowledge Mya on her birthday. He slipped out from underneath Valencia's arm and into their empty living room to send Mya a text.

"Welcome to life after 21."

He waited a few minutes to see if Mya would respond. As he waited, he thought about the empty room that surrounded him. He thought about why he did it in the first place. He had a plan — a sure one as far as he was concerned. He hadn't even attempted to purchase divorce papers. In January, he was certain that he and Valencia would be living separately by now. He and Mya could then move in together and take their relationship from hit-and-miss to a bona fide family. Instead, things between Don and Mya had slowed down and things between he and Valencia were getting cozier.

Nonetheless, Don realized that he was the only one to blame. If he hadn't allowed anyone (namely his mother) to persuade him otherwise, he would be done with Valencia by now. But, then there was Mya. How could she ever have a relationship with someone that her family would never approve of?

Mya texted Don back.

"Call me! Tell me about this life you speak of. Lol"

Don smiled and pressed the talk button on his phone.

"Hello," Mya said.

"You sound like you're half sleep," Don said.

"How come I can't sound half awake?" Mya asked.

"This isn't an optimism-pessimism argument. When did it ever become a negative thing to be awaken from sleep when your boyfriend texts you on your birthday?" Don asked.

"Okay, I wasn't prepared to argue that so you win."

"Thank you. You have so much to learn on this side of twenty-one."

"You're only twenty-four!"

"Yes, and until recently, I was three years older than you."

"For what? Four whole days?"

"Hey now. Every moment counts."

"You were two when I was born."

"And you were still twenty the day I turned twenty-three."

"For four days!"

"If the world ended yesterday, how old would you have been?"

"Twenty-one point nine nine nine nine."

Don laughed. "That is ridiculous. Easily the most sophomoric thing you've said post twenty-one."

"For real?" Mya asked.

"For real, for real."

"I've got one better."

"Shoot."

"I haven't seen you since I was twenty-one."

Don laughed. "I don't even know why I laughed. That was super dumb."

"So now it's dumb to miss my boyfriend?" Mya teased.

"You said it, not me. What do you have planned?"

"I plan on hanging out with you."

"Can't."

"Why not?"

"I'm seeing someone."

Mya wasn't sure if he was serious, but she bit anyway.

"Who is she?" Mya asked.

"You don't know her," Don said.

"She must be someone special."

"She is. It's her birthday so we're hanging out."

"Where?"

"Her choice."

Mya picked up that Don was referring to her.

"Oh really? She probably wants you to meet her at her apartment," Mya said.

"Probably," Don said.

"I bet she just wants to lay in bed and talk. Maybe get a little something overnight."

"You're probably right."

"Lucky girl. Is she pretty?"

"More than that."

"Sounds like you really like this one."

"Something like that."

"I'm sure she knows that, but when was the last time you told her that?"

Don paused for a moment. He realized that he hadn't told Mya he loved her in a while. Anytime she said it to him, he would reply arrogantly with, 'That's what you say'. Those words would sting Mya as if he slapped her. Don never took note about how those words affected her. At first, he wanted Mya to forget about him. It would have been the best thing for her. But, the longer she stuck around and put up with his bullshit, the more attached he became to her. Now, he never wanted her to leave. But, in case she woke up one day and decided that enough was enough, he had Valencia as his backup plan. In Mya's eyes, though, Mya was the backup plan. She just held out hope that one day she wouldn't be.

Don suddenly hung up the phone. Mya lay in bed perplexed at his reaction. She wondered if it had something to do with either Millie or Valencia. She waited to see if her phone would ring. It did. But, it was just a text. It was from Don.

"I love you, Mya Brown. I promise to fix this. I just need a little more time. I'll see you later."

Chapter 54

Wednesday, December 24, 2008

Mya had many reasons to celebrate. She was one semester from completing the registered nurse program at SMU. Cathy Shields all but guaranteed her a job at Parkland, granted that she passed all the necessary certification tests. Brenda was retiring within the next few years and Cathy was set on having Mya groomed to replace Brenda as head nurse. And, although Mya had been demoted from leading lady in Don's life, they were still a couple after one year.

Don promised Mya that he wouldn't miss their night together for anything in the world. She was excited to see Don. That night she was going to give Don a five-year plan about how things were going to work between them. She was great at planning and even better at executing a plan. Mya prefaced their meeting with a promise of a big surprise. Don had a surprise of his own.

Mya had been at the Highland Hotel since about 5:30 that evening. She was trying on different lingerie pieces she had purchased earlier that month. They were more for her than for Don. The lingerie made her feel sexy. In the end, she knew Don was going to tear it off of her like wrapping paper on a highly-anticipated present.

Around 6:20, there was a knock on the door. Mya assumed that it was Don trying to surprise her by being early. He wasn't supposed to be there until 7. Mya quickly grabbed a robe to conceal what she was wearing.

"Just a minute," Mya called out as she walked to the door and tied the belt on the bathrobe. She opened the door and immediately regretted it once she saw who it was.

"What are you doing here, Jason?" Mya asked the white, middle-aged man in a blazer and some trousers, standing at the door.

"Is that how you greet your loyal bodyguard these days?" Jason asked.

"You work for my father. Not me," Mya corrected.

Jason had been on detail since the day Mya was born. Senator Brown hired Jason Foreman after he was fired from the police department for allegedly fatally shooting an unarmed black man who ran from the scene of a murder. It was later determined that the man Foreman shot was not involved in the murder. Senator Brown felt that Foreman should have been reinstated after the investigation came back inconclusive. Yet, a report from a higher-ranking officer that described Foreman as 'a loose cannon' was enough to keep him from returning to the force after only an eight-year stint.

Mya, at one point, referred to Foreman as Uncle Jason until Jason informed Mya that friendships go further than family ties, and that friends do favors for one another. Therefore, five-year-old Mya did Jason a favor by not telling her father about Jason sleeping in the same bed as his mother while her father was away. Jason did fourteen-year-old Mya a favor by covering for her when she snuck out her window to meet her high school crush at the movies. The favors game between them went back and forth.

The game had escalated recently. Mya's grade point average had dipped below the allowable minimum for one of her scholarships shortly after Don told her that Valencia was expecting. To cover the remaining costs for the current semester, Mya asked Jason to forge a check in her father's name. Jason obliged. Therefore, Jason saw an opportunity to up the ante. He showed up at her apartment late one night. Jason drank himself into a stupor as he waited for Don to leave and then knocked on Mya's door. When she invited him in, he pounced on her and demanded that she have sex with him in return. Mya couldn't believe it, but she feared the consequences of rejecting him. Therefore, she lay there motionless as he inserted his penis in her and attempted to kiss her tight-lipped mouth. Fortunately for Mya, the encounter didn't last long. Less than one minute.

Seeing Jason on that night of all nights was a bad omen in Mya's superstitious eyes, and reminded her of a night she wished she could forget.

"You're right, Mya. I work for your father. But, I was in the area and I thought you would like a gander at this information. Or, maybe I should take this file I found on your boyfriend directly to Senator Brown instead of talking to you," Jason said.

"Wait!" Mya said then sighed heavily. She opened the door wider to invite Jason in.

"That's what I thought. You know, you've really turned out to be quite the woman. Who would have known?" Jason commented as he entered the room.

"What do you want?" Mya asked.

"I'm a fan of the last arrangement we made."

"You're sick."

"And your boyfriend is a thug."

"At least he doesn't have a thing for girls less than half his age. How bad could it be?"

"It's all in this file," Jason said as he held up a brown folder. "Trust me. Our exchange will be totally even. Has Uncle Jason ever let you down?"

Chapter 55

Don made it to the hotel at 6:23. He made his way to the front desk and was handed a hotel key by the man stationed there. The hotel clerk was the type to never forget a face or a matching pair. Once the clerk recognized Mya, he kept an eye out for Don.

Don smiled to himself and made a mental note to tip the clerk handsomely the next time he saw him. He made his way up to the room and attempted to sneak into room nine-eighteen undetected. However, when he opened the door he heard a man's voice. He entered the room and saw a white male bending over to pull up his pants from his ankles. Don didn't catch what he was saying. He did see (what looked to be) Mya's legs spread at the edge of the bed directly in front of where the man was standing. Don exited the room unnoticed, but he let the door close on its own. The shutting door caused Jason and Mya to snap to attention.

Don took the elevator to the ground floor and nearly passed the front desk. But, he remembered his intentions and handed the clerk a fifty-dollar tip. He then went outside to gather his thoughts. He didn't want to get in his vehicle yet because he wasn't sure if he could drive in that state of mind. He realized that he still had the room key in his pocket, but he wasn't sure if he wanted to turn it in and leave or go back upstairs. He finally became aware of the chill in the air and decided to go back inside.

In passing, he saw the same white man from the room walking through the foyer towards the exit. They exchanged glares as Don walked to the elevators. He didn't hurry back to the room. He didn't know what to expect when he reentered the room and he was already at a loss for words. Instead of using his key, he knocked.

Mya opened the door. She was clutching a document in her hand and her face was tear-streaked. Neither of them said anything. Don just fearlessly stared into Mya's eyes. Mya was searching his face for a sign of someone that she thought she knew.

"So," Mya prompted.

"So?" Don asked.

"Who are you?" Mya asked.

"The same person who walked in on you and the mysterious, old man not too long ago," Don said.

"Don't you turn this around on me."

"Oh, so you're a saint because you think you're not as bad as you think I am? I get it."

"Don...wait, what is your name again?"

"Adonis Lane."

"Legally?"

"You can say that."

"How about Marquis Lane?"

"What about him?"

"That's you, isn't it?"

Don didn't answer.

"It sure looks like you. Well, a younger version of you," Mya said. "Same birthday. Same scar on the left side. Same chipped tooth."

"Your point?" Don asked.

"This is you!" Mya said referring to the document in her hand.

"Was me. Allegedly."

"So, you did it?"

Again, Don offered no answer.

"Look around, Don. Look at where you are. No lies. That was our pact. Do you remember that?" Mya asked.

"Technically, I'm not inside the room," Don said.

"Real mature, Don. Why not show me some respect and answer me?"

"I can't."

"So, you did do it. You killed those four people?"

"Mya, please do not ask me questions that you do not want the answer to."

"I knew it! I knew it was too good to be true."

"Don't do that. You're better than that."

"Do what? Have regrets?" Mya asked.

"Look. There is no statute of limitations on murder. What I say can be used against me...or others," Don explained.

"So, you don't trust me. That's what that means."

"Can I trust you? After what I just saw?"

"What did you see?"

"Man, I ain't about to play games with you."

"He was blackmailing me, Don!"

"Who is he?"

"My dad's bodyguard."

"I knew I've seen him before!"

"You know my dad?"

Don sighed and related to Mya as much as he was willing to reveal. Mya's father retired from the police department to pursue a career in politics and law. When Don was thirteen, Senator Brown's close friend pegged Don as one of the suspects in a series of home invasions. During one of those home invasions, a group of four teens were murdered. The key witness in the case gave four different stories before trial, and, as a result, the charges against Adonis Marquis Lane (who cops listed as Marquis Lane in their files) were dropped until more evidence could be gathered or better witnesses could be found.

However, Senator Brown was not satisfied. He pulled a few strings with people in power and essentially had the troubled teen ran out of town. In what amounted to an excommunication, Don was to never return to the Dallas area or he would face the threat of being thrown in jail and tried for the deaths of those four teens.

Mya was hurt that Don didn't trust her with that information before that day.

"Why didn't you tell me that you knew my father?" Mya asked.

"I didn't know he was your father until the day we ran into him at the play," Don said. "By then, it was too late."

"Too late?"

"I was in love with you by then."

"Was?"

"Yeah...was."

"So, you're no longer in love with me?"

"Look, Mya. This is a mistake."

"No. Come in here and tell me that."

"How much time can you buy me?"

"Two weeks, maybe three."

"I should be gone by then."

"So, you're leaving?" Mya asked.

"I have a daughter to protect," Don said.

"What am I supposed to do when you leave?"

"Do you."

"Do me?"

"Yeah. Do whatever you choose."

"Like seeing other guys? Sleeping with other guys?"

"If that's what you want to do, do it."

"And you don't care? I'm not going to wait for you if you leave, Don. I've waited for you long enough," Mya said.

"Fine," Don said.

Mya grabbed Don by the hand and pulled him into the room. The door closed behind him. Don knew what was coming, but Mya had already been warned.

"Tell me now," Mya said.

"I'm not in love with you anymore, Mya." Don said without hesitating. He then walked out of the room without looking back.

Chapter 56

Tuesday, January 13, 2009

Valencia was inexplicably happy about moving to Florida. She was happier about getting away from the competition — namely, Mya. Donna Lane was sad that there would be considerable distance between her and Emilia. Emilia brought the best out of everyone who knew her. Donna's health seemed to improve with Emilia's arrival. Cathy was going to miss her too. She knew about Don's alleged past. She never asked if the accusations were true. She didn't need to know. Her mind was already set on his innocence. Cathy was more sad for Mya than Mya seemed.

Mya went on with business as usual. She had a degree to finish. There was nothing she could do to change Don's mind and, to Mya, that was evidence that he chose Valencia over her. In public, she seemed indifferent. However, behind closed doors, everything around Mya reminded her of Don. Articles of clothing. Pictures. Her phone. The radio. The side of the bed he slept on. The apartment itself. It was all too much. Thus, she stayed away from her own apartment.

Mya never skipped clinicals, but Don had texted her out of nowhere, requesting that she pick him up from his apartment. Don had sold his vehicle in preparation for the move east. She complied with his request and took him to her apartment. It was raining that day. Don brought his PlayStation 2 with him and suggested they spend the day battling it out on a NCAA Football game. They used to always compete on video games. Most of the time it was Nintendo Wii.

Don set up the game for them and uploaded all the cheats in his favor. Don's competitive spirit always caused him to look for an unfair advantage. For instance, one day, he and Mya were playing a bowling game on her Nintendo Wii. Don wasn't doing bad, but Mya was bowling a perfect game. So, right before the sixth frame, Don pulled down Mya's pants and panties, bent her over the back of the couch, and fucked Mya from behind. The sudden quickie threw her off balance and ruined her perfect game.

This time, Mya had no idea about the cheats, yet she suggested that they wager 'the usual' — oral sex. Don agreed. At halftime, Mya conceded that Don was the clear winner. The score was 108-0.

Mya tossed her controller aside and hungrily stared at the man sitting beside her on the bed. She tried convincing Don to put the game away by putting his dick in her mouth. It didn't take long. Don undressed Mya and got underneath the covers with her. He entered Mya and took it slow with her. Don immediately thought about a conversation they had earlier in their relationship. Mya was considering having a baby with Don at the start of their relationship. Don talked her out of it, but now he was regretting it. He knew he couldn't remain a relevant concern to Mya if he was hundreds of miles away. A baby would give him an excuse to find a way to stay in her life. With that thought in mind, he looked into Mya's eyes.

"This is your last chance to get pregnant," Don said softly.

Mya gave a quick smile, but was she concentrating on adjusting to Don's size as he delivered each stroke. Mya held on to him tightly and let her body tell him that she still loved him and that she missed him already. Despite what Don said with his words, his body reciprocated the message. Mya received the message clear as day.

Mya hardly took time to notice that Don was cuddling with her afterward. She couldn't stand facing away from him. She lay with him on the same pillow, forehead to forehead, as she watched herself play with his hand and kiss his fingers. She was trying to keep herself from crying. Don turned over on his back and pulled her closer. She laid her head on his shoulder. He played with her hair. She liked when he played with her hair. Mya became anxious. She felt as if the time she had with him was escaping, so she climbed on top of Don and said,

"One more time. After that, I'll let you go."

Chapter 57

Friday, February 20, 2009

By the next evening, Don, Valencia, and Emilia were in Orlando, Florida. They settled into an apartment at the West Oaks Apartment complex about two miles away from where Don worked a new job at Lowe's Home Improvement Store on West Colonial Drive.

Unfortunately, his hours as an inventory handler clashed with Valencia's hours as a pharmacy technician. And since the CVS that she worked at was much further away, she needed the car to drive to her job. Moreover, she was responsible for making sure Emilia got to and from daycare — Valencia's cousin's house. Most of Emilia's extended family lived in Florida. That thought made Don uncomfortable and happy at the same time. He felt outnumbered, yet he was relieved to have help with Valencia's problem.

As if scheduled, Valencia had another cutting episode on February 13th. It wasn't as bad, but it was just as stressful because Don didn't know what triggered it.

He hadn't talked to Mya on the phone since he left Texas. They rarely kept in touch via email. Don changed his number at Valencia's request and told Mya that his phone was cut off. He had no intentions of trying to nurse a long-distance relationship. If she had an affair, it would be easy to hide and easy to lie about certain things. He had forgiven her, but the hurt hadn't subsided yet. That being said, he didn't feel the need to invite more potential heartache. Not when he could avoid it.

Don immersed himself into the new routine he called life. He tried focusing on making a life for Millie and not taking for granted the time he had with her. It seemed she was learning new words daily, and although she was not quite two, he purchased a reading program that encourages reading amongst infants and toddlers to help her progress.

Emilia knew who she was to her daddy. He seemed to always give in to any request she made, even as her mother protested. She had been saying 'daddy' well before she said 'mama'. Don believed that she could, but she just wasn't fond of her mother.

Don just happened to have a day off. With only eight days left in the month, Don wondered where the time had gone. He spent the day reading and playing with Emilia and touching base with his mother, Donna. He called Cathy as well. She hinted that something was going on with Mya. Don decided to see if Mya had attempted to contact him via email.

There it was. It was dated January 29, 2009, but Don had neglected to even check it. Don focused on two words in the entire message:

I'm pregnant.

At first, Don dismissed it, and (while in that mindset) replied to Mya's message skeptically. He didn't question her being pregnant. He questioned the timing because he felt like she wouldn't likely test positive until the third week. Not sixteen days. His words. Further, Mya said something that Don would hold against her for years:

"I'm not going to wait for you if you leave, Don. I've waited for you long enough."

He took that as a clear indication that she would start sleeping with other men.

On the other hand, the timing was perfect. Don chose to move the day after he planned to have unprotected sex with Mya one last time. Don knew Mya better than she ever realized. He knew that when she found out about his alleged past, their relationship would be over. So, Don planned on leaving Mya something to remember him by. He timed her period and estimated the peak of her ovulation cycle — January thirteenth. If his plan worked, the baby was actually his. Now he needed to know just how pregnant she was.

Chapter 58

Tuesday, May 19, 2009 — Dallas, TX

Don made sure he wasn't late to Mya's graduation ceremony. Shortly after finding out she was pregnant, Don gave Mya his new number. They discreetly texted back and forth at Don's request. He didn't want to seem too tied to his phone and make Valencia suspicious of his activities. He was only supposed to give his number to family he could trust. But, keeping in contact with Mya was a must.

Besides possibly being pregnant with Don's child, Mya balanced him out with her caring personality. She cared if he had a good day at work. She knew his schedule and never forgot to text Don the minute his shift ended. She was always the first and sometimes the only person to ask about how his day went. He didn't realize how much that meant to him until he talked to Mya on a regular basis.

Mya knew what the circumstances of him leaving were. But, she couldn't fight the urge to invite Don to share in a day that meant so much to her. Graduation day. A day of pride, accomplishment, and sharing that moment with loved ones. She didn't actually expect Don to come, but she was overwhelmed with excitement when he said he would.

Don arranged to arrive in Dallas a day early to spend time with his mother. Meanwhile, Mya arranged to celebrate with her family the day before graduation so she wouldn't be too exhausted by trying to fit it all into one day. Her words. Truth was, she intended on meeting up with Don after her graduation. However, since Mya pulled the pregnancy card, her family understood and they respected her wishes. Although they were not happy about Mya being pregnant by Don, they were supportive of her having the baby and were excited about welcoming a new member of the family.

Don disguised himself as a SMU student. He wore a Mustang ball cap and a red SMU t-shirt. Instead of sitting among the families of the graduating students, he sat among the current students who sought inspiration and motivation to complete their conquest. Mya had no idea where Don was, but she could feel he was near. She had to prevent herself from looking for him. Anytime someone blurted out randomly, she used it as an excuse to look in that direction to see if she could find him. She didn't see him until she walked across stage. He made sure to jump out of his seat when she surveyed the crowd as she waved to her family. He was out of her parents' view, but he grabbed Mya's attention. Mya couldn't see his eyes because of the brim of his hat, but she knew that smile.

After the ceremony, Don positioned himself where he could see Mya, but she couldn't see him. He wanted to congratulate her there, but thought better of it when he saw Foreman. Instead, he sent her a text saying that he would meet her at her apartment.

The night didn't go as planned. At least not in Mya's eyes. Don was somewhat standoffish. He acted as if he didn't know Mya as well as he did. He wouldn't lie next to her at first and when he did, he kept moving his hand whenever she put it on her stomach. He didn't reference the baby at all. Mya wanted to have sex, but Don acted as if he wasn't interested. He used the I-don't-want-to-hurt-you excuse.

Mya thought he may have been drinking, but all he had with him was a couple of sports drinks. He claimed that he gave up drinking alcohol. She tasted his drinks when he went to the bathroom to be sure. No alcohol. However, she liked the taste of it so much that she kept grabbing it and taking a sip. Don took note.

Mya wanted Don to see her belly progressively grow as the pregnancy went on. Therefore, she told him about her plans to spend the summer in Orlando. Don didn't react to the news. He just asked where she planned on staying. Mya revealed that Lisa was attending UCF and that she had an apartment near campus. Don thought it was strange that she and Lisa had reconciled, but he commented it was typical of women. However, Don was surprised to learn that Mya would be in Orlando in two days.

Chapter 59

Friday, May 22, 2009

Mya was too tired to venture out, yet she was too bored to stay still. She was waiting for Don to get off work so she could text him that she had arrived earlier than she expected. Lisa was at work, which meant that Mya was alone in the apartment. Lisa left Mya a key, but she knew nothing about the area and didn't want to risk getting lost — even with GPS in her rental.

Mya decided that the best way to satisfy her craving for fresh air would be to take a walk around the apartment complex. She stepped outside and studied the landmarks and the building number. Then she scanned the surrounding area and began exploring.

She noticed that the people were friendly towards her. She figured it had to do with the fact she was pregnant and showing. However, she realized that even people that seemed to be in a hurry were kind enough to make sure that they didn't bump into her. She was starting to believe it was a way of life — contrary to what she heard about people who lived out east.

Welcome to Florida, Mya thought.

After meandering for about twenty minutes, Mya made her way back to the front of Lisa's building. Before going back inside, Mya decided to take a seat on the stairs and watch cars go by on the busy street nearby. That's when she saw Lisa's car pull into the parking lot and park. Lisa trotted to Mya as if she was in a semi-hurry.

"What's the rush?" Mya asked.

"I got someone waiting for me in the car. That's all," Lisa said.

"Where are you going?" Mya inquired.

"To grab some lunch. Then back to work. I would invite you to lunch but—" Lisa said then subtly gestured to the car.

Mya looked past Lisa over to the car and caught a glimpse of Valencia looking at herself in the side view mirror on the passenger's side.

"Oh my gosh! Is that?" Mya couldn't say it.

"Yeah," Lisa confirmed.

"Don't move! Let me stand up and go inside before she notices me."

Fortunately for Mya, Lisa was blocking Valencia's view of her. Mya quickly stood and briskly made her way into Lisa's apartment. Lisa followed.

"Does she know I'm here?" Mya asked.

"No. I didn't expect you to be outside. I tried to buy you some time by parking on the other side of the lot," Lisa said.

"Do you think she saw me?"

"No. I don't know. I doubt it."

"Don would kill me. He would think I did it on purpose."

"Yeah. If he wasn't so hot, I would hate him for playing my friends against each other."

Mya ignored the compliment she paid Don. Only because she knew that Lisa was not Don's type, so there was no chance of him cheating on Mya and Valencia with Lisa. Her words.

"It's not like he got me pregnant on purpose," Mya said.

"True, but still," Lisa said.

"Look. I can't demand that you not be friends with her. But, while I'm here, I would appreciate it if me and her didn't encounter each other."

"Are you asking me not to bring her over here?"

"Yes."

"Done. Can I go now?"

"Wait! She doesn't know I'm pregnant."

"What? That is so wrong."

"And you're a saint?"

"Point taken."

"Don is supposed to tell her. So, can you not mention that I'm here? Or prego?"

"I'm sure I can manage that."

"Thanks."

"No problem."

Lisa grabbed some money off the mantel and jogged back to her car.

"Why so long?" Valencia asked teasingly.

"Oh. Sorry. My friend wasn't feeling well," Lisa said.

"She sick?" Valencia asked.

"Yeah. She's pregnant," Lisa explained.

"Aw. A baby. Have we met? Maybe we make shower for her."

"Maybe. Too soon at the moment. Let's go eat."

Chapter 60

Thursday, May 28, 2009 — 6:28AM

Mya was ill. But, she was always ill at that time every morning. Morning sickness was part of her daily routine. Her phone had awakened her. It was ringing. Don was calling.

"Hello?" Mya answered.

"You coming today?" Don asked.

"Yeah," Mya replied.

"If not, I can walk. But, I need to know now," Don said.

"No, I'll be there."

"I'm ready." Don hung up.

As soon as Don ended the call, she hurried to the bathroom to vomit. She wouldn't miss that part of summer at all. The only thing good about being up at that hour was it meant that she got to see Don before he went to work. She had incorporated a half hour block for Don in her daily routine. She fit that in after brushing her teeth and before going to

Chick-fil-A. On the way to Don's apartment complex, she would eat a banana for breakfast.

She and Don arrived at the Lowe's on West Colonial Drive at 7:40 — twenty minutes before Don's shift started. Mya usually parked near the entrance, but that day she parked towards the back of the parking lot where the employees parked. She looked at Don and gave him a familiar smile. Don knew she was going to try something. In prior conversations, she talked about how she was often aroused and was constantly urging Don to relieve her sexual tension. That morning, though, Don could see a remnant of the banana she had earlier on her gums. He imagined it could be vomit and decided to distract her with conversation.

"Where is the Powerade I left in here yesterday?" Don asked.

"I drank it," Mya said.

"You drank it?" Don asked.

"Yeah. It was yummy! I think the baby liked it too," Mya said.

"I doubt the baby cares at this point."

"I don't know. That's one of the few things I can add to my list of food and drink that he or she doesn't make me spew back up."

"You still vomit every day?"

"Yeah."

"It looks like you forgot to wash your mouth out. You got something behind your top lip."

Mya pulled down her visor to look in the small mirror.

"No, that's my breakfast. I was saving that for later," Mya said.

She laughed. Don didn't.

"That's gross," Don said. Banana breath was just as bad as having vomit breath to Don.

"Hey now. Our baby likes it."

"I hate bananas."

"Well he or she takes after mommy."

"When are you going to find out the sex of your baby."

"Our baby."

"The baby is definitely yours. The donor has yet to be determined."

"Ass!"

"I'm just saying."

"Anyway, I had an appointment back home, but since I'm down here, Cathy made some calls so I can be seen at a clinic down here on the seventeenth."

"Why couldn't you just say the seventeenth? Why did you have to give me the background and the entire story? I didn't ask all that," Don teased.

"You are such an ass," Mya said smiling.

"Anyway, you owe me a Powerade."

"For real?" Mya asked while leaning towards Don.

"For real, for real," Don said right before engaging in a long kiss with Mya.

"If that's the case, you owe me some dick."

"For taxi services?"

"Yeah, for starters."

"Oh, I see. You're looking for a *tip*, baby?" Don asked seductively.

"Yeah," Mya answered. She anticipated Don initiating a quickie.

"Clean out the trash on the floor before you return the car. Rental places appreciate that."

Chapter 61

Tuesday, June 9, 2009

Don was stretched out on the bed with his laptop in front of him. Valencia entered the room from the master bathroom, straddled him, lay on his back, and looked over his shoulder.

"Don-Don, you no leave yet?" Valencia asked.

The time was 8:05. Valencia assumed that Don was supposed to be at work by eight that day. He wasn't. His shift started later that morning.

"Nope. I quit," Don teased.

"What are you doing?" Valencia asked.

"Checking on my blog, checking my email, minding my business," Don said.

"So mean."

"Did I hurt your feelings?"

"If I say yes?"

"I'll make it up to you."

"How?"

"What do you want?" Don asked.

"Roll over and I show you," Valencia said.

Valencia went back to straddling Don on her knees. Don turned over onto his back and saw that Valencia was wearing only panties.

"I thought I felt naked tits on my back," Don said.

Valencia laughed. "So silly."

"Let me guess. You want to smother me with those."

"You like me to?"

"Well, that's one way to die."

"I give mouth to mouth."

Valencia lay on top of Don, kissed him, and clutched his dick. Don reached for his laptop. Valencia pushed it out of his reach. Don suddenly flipped Valencia onto her back and covered her breasts with a pillow.

"Tiny footsteps," Don whispered.

Emilia burst into the room instantly.

"Daddy!" Emilia exclaimed.

"Hey, Boobie. Are you ready for daycare?" Don asked.

"I go to work with you, Daddy," Emilia said.

"Is that so?" Don asked.

"Yes," Emilia said.

"Then what is Daddy going to do?" Don asked.

"You go to work and I go to work," Emilia said.

"Then who's going to daycare?" Don asked.

"Mom-mom," Emilia said.

Valencia laughed.

"No. She can't," Don said.

"Um...Bevo?" Emilia suggested referring to her favorite stuffed teddy bear.

"Bevo can't go by himself. I tell you what, you go to work and Daddy will go to daycare with Bevo. Okay?" Don said.

"No, I go with you and Bevo," Emilia said.

"One of us has to go work, Millie," Don said.

Emilia thought about it. "Okay. You go to work. I go get your keys for you, Daddy." She ran out of the room.

Don turned to Valencia. "I guess I'm going to work. No daycare for me." He reached under the pillow Valencia was holding to her chest, grabbed a handful of breast, and squeezed.

"Hey! That teet belong to my honey," Valencia said with a smile.

"Well, he'll probably hate this too."

Don gently pinched Valencia on the pussy. When she flinched, he pinched her on the ass. She moved her hands and he pinched her on the breast. Valencia laughed.

"My honey kick your butt when he catch you," Valencia said then laughed. She followed his hands with hers to block future pinches. She couldn't. Don was too fast for her.

"Well, I'm going to get you until he gets here," Don said.

Don continued his light pinching.

"Okay, okay! You my honey! You my honey!"

"Are you sure?"

"Jes!"

Don quit pinching. "Oh. So, what do I do, now?"

"Kick your ass," Valencia said with a smile and then laughed.

Don walked to work listening to music on his phone. A few random Chris Brown songs played during that walk, which made him think of Mya. He planned on talking to her later that night.

Don didn't stay at work long. Maybe three hours. He got a text on his phone from Valencia.

"She's pregnant!"

Oh shit! Don thought. *How did she found out?*

Don located his supervisor and informed him that it was vital that he go home immediately. Don had a good name with the managers there. They didn't hesitate to give him the rest of the day off if he needed it. Don clocked out and started his trek home. He texted Valencia when he was within a block of the apartment.

"What are you talking about?" Don texted.

"That girl! I see your email." Valencia texted back.

"Fuck!" Don said aloud to himself. He got so caught up with fooling around with Valencia that he forgot to close his email.

He called Valencia.

"Hello," Valencia answered. Don could hear her sniffling as if she was crying.

"Valencia. Why are you crying?" Don asked.

"You get her pregnant," Valencia said.

"How? I'm here with you," Don said.

"She say it's you."

"Yeah, I know."

"I hear wind. Where are you?"

"In the parking lot."

"Here?"

"Yeah, I'm coming in."

"No!"

"Why not?"

"Stay outside, Don-Don!"

Don froze in place on the sidewalk outside of the apartment.

"Okay. Talk to me," Don said.

"Is it yours?" Valencia asked.

"I don't know."

"You don't know? I thought you no see her."

"I made a mistake right before we moved here. She has someone else. I think she's trying to make me jealous."

"Why?"

"I don't know."

"You love her?"

"What? Come on, Valencia."

"She loves you. She say it in email."

"I know."

"What you do now, Don-Don?"

"What do you want me to do?"

"Fix it! Or lose me and Millie!"

Chapter 62

Thursday, June 11, 2009

Don didn't get much sleep Wednesday night. He was sweating over a scheme he put into play the day before. He had rather the reason he couldn't sleep be because Valencia was hounding him all night. It wasn't though. He was one word from sleeping on the couch. Well, Valencia didn't have enough backbone to do that. She feared Don in more ways than one. But, she felt as if she had enough leverage with the alleged pregnancy to pull it off. She rejected Don's affectionate touches. She didn't want to. She needed to so she could keep the upper hand.

Don, though, was desperate. He didn't talk to Mya on Tuesday — the day Valencia found out about the baby. He had to play it safe. Valencia told Don her take on it.

Fix it.

He couldn't live life without Millie.

It hit him like ton of bricks Tuesday night. Don jumped out of bed. He couldn't live life without Millie.

He was seemingly calm, but acting irrationally. He went into the kitchen and grabbed a couple of Powerade drinks. One grape flavor and the other strawberry lemonade. He broke the seals on both and sipped out of them.

He couldn't live life without Millie.

He searched through the cabinets underneath the sink and pulled out a clear, liquid insecticide. He added some to the grape Powerade. He paused when he came to the other one.

Purple, right?

He closed them both and put them back into the refrigerator. Then he went to bed.

He couldn't live life without Millie.

The next morning, Don got into Mya's car with his drinks in hand on the way to work. Mya was happy to see him, but he was quiet. He failed to mention the email discovery. More like he intentionally withheld that information from Mya. When they made it to his workplace, Don initiated the sexual contact with Mya. He kissed her, got her all worked up, and then abruptly exited the car. He left behind the grape Powerade.

His actions were causing him to lose sleep. He hadn't heard from Mya since he saw her Wednesday morning. No text asking about work. Nothing. He was nervous because in less than two hours, she was supposed to be there. *If* she made it.

If God wants her and the baby to make it, He'll save her, Don thought.

Don sent Mya a text at 6:20. She responded fifteen minutes later, citing being sicker than usual as her reason for the late response. Don's adrenaline level spiked.

What did I do?

Mya arrived at the apartment complex ten minutes later than usual, but she was still early enough to get Don to work on time. Don looked at Mya cautiously. He was concerned, but he didn't want to seem alarmed. The bottle of Powerade was missing. Don was certain of it. He had been looking for it since he got into the car.

Mya looked miserable. She tried to smile through her agony. Don didn't say much during the short drive. He just stared out the window and gave short responses to her conversation. They arrived in the parking lot; however, instead of parking, Mya pulled up to the entrance.

"Are you going to be okay?" Don asked.

"I hope so," Mya said.

"Call me if you need me," Don said.

"Okay, I need you. Now what?" Mya replied.

"Seriously?"

"I'll be fine."

Don started to get out.

"Oh, before I forget, you left your drink in here yesterday. It's underneath the seat," Mya said.

Don retrieved it and saw that it was still full.

"I'm surprised you didn't drink it," Don said. He was fishing.

"I would have, but it's the purple kind."

"I thought purple was your favorite color?"

"It is, but I like the pink kind you had."

Don kissed Mya. It was a long, soft kiss — a kiss that they hadn't shared since they were both back in Texas.

Don was relieved. He took the laced bottle with him and poured out the poisonous contents in the restroom sink. He caught a glimpse of himself in the mirror. A single tear spoke volumes. God had answered him.

The baby was meant to be.

Chapter 63

Wednesday, June 17, 2009

In less than a week, Don had turned the tables on Valencia. He made Valencia feel like the pregnancy was her fault. Had she not driven Don away with her indiscretions, there wouldn't have been the slightest possibility. And as things stood, there was no proof that Don acknowledged the baby as his own. Thus, he demanded that Valencia drop the issue and concentrate on being a family with him and Emilia.

Valencia tabled the issue for the moment in fear that Don might try to sever the relationship for good. Valencia wasn't stupid. She knew that there was more than a slim chance that Don had fathered a baby with Mya. In fact, she thought she imagined seeing a pregnant version of Mya nearly two months prior. She figured now that woman served as a vision or omen of news to come.

Valencia believed that Mya was in Texas.

Don was at work when he got the news. He and Mya would welcome a boy into the world. His short spell of excitement was followed by a sense of dread. The situation made him think about Diana and Dejahmi all over again. If he became attached to the new baby and the baby didn't make it, Don would be crushed. Don wasn't superstitious, but he felt that he got everything that he didn't ask for and nothing that he hoped for. Maybe if he didn't act too excited, Fate would allow him to get something he actually wanted. His words.

Mya was already set on a first name for the baby. Ethan — which means strong. Don passively negotiated, but he didn't insist that he name their son. Don named Emilia. Mya left the middle name completely up to Don, but Don felt as if he was limited. There weren't many meaningful names that fit with Ethan. His words. He wasn't crazy about the first name either. He just thought it was too common. His children were to be unique.

Don was watching highlights of an old football game when he saw a name he liked. Darius. The name came from a running back of a small school in Nevada. When Don looked up the meaning of the name online, he liked it even better. He texted Mya his choice for a middle name.

"What does it mean?" Mya texted.

"Why do you assume I know?" Don texted back.

"Because I know you?" Mya texted in reply.

"You might know me a little bit. Sound familiar?" Don texted.

"Tell me or I'm going to look it up."

"Look it up."

"Donnie!"

"Okay! It means upholder of good."

Chapter 64

Saturday, June 20, 2009

Valencia spent all morning trying to dig up something on Mya. She wanted to know where Mya was, whom she talked to, and every guy she slept with. Her words. Valencia assumed that she could get that information and more from Facebook. Unfortunately for Valencia, Mya's page was private. There was very little for her to go on since they weren't friends. Valencia looked to see what friends they did have in common. Three. One of which was Lisa. Don, however, was not one of them. Valencia took pride in knowing that her man was not secretly keeping up with a young fling.

Valencia then looked for wall-to-wall conversation between Lisa and Mya. Nothing revealing. Nothing recent either. It was as if Mya didn't exist to the people Valencia associated with on a regular basis. She went back to Mya's page to find a clue. Rich had recently commented on Mya's profile picture. Valencia had deleted Rich as a friend a while ago so he hadn't popped up as a common friend. Rich's page was not private, yet she doubted that she would find what she was looking for. However, the writing was on the wall.

Mya brought Rich up to speed about her pregnancy. They talked about the due date; joked about weight gain; talked about Don being in Florida; and discussed the baby's name. Mya plainly made a statement about how she loved the middle name Don chose — Darius. She went on about the name being thoughtful and how she hoped that Don and Ethan Darius have a close relationship.

Valencia found the information heartbreaking and seconds after she read it, the news became pride-shattering; she saw that her lunch buddy gave the news a "Like".

Valencia focused her attention on Lisa and called her immediately.

"Hello, bestie," Lisa answered.

"Hello, bitch," Valencia replied.

"Excuse me?" Lisa rebutted.

"Yeah you-you eh-stupid bitch! You no tell me about Don-Don baby! Why?" Valencia said.

"It's not my place. I thought he told you."

"No, he no tell me. He tell me he no think the baby his."

"Really? She is *not* a ho."

"She loves Don-Don, no?"

"Yeah. She really does."

"You think it Don-Don baby?"

"I know it is."

"She have no boyfriend?"

"Don *is* her boyfriend. But you need to take that up with him."

"No! He mine, bitch! You tell that bitch that too!"

"Watch it, Valencia! You don't know who you're messing with."

"Don-Don no want that baby. He wants me and Millie. You tell her," Valencia said.

"Don loves Mya! I hate to be the one that breaks it to ya!" Lisa said.

"If he love her, why he no with her?"

"Coz you're crazy! He can't trust that you won't take his baby girl away from him! That's why!"

Valencia didn't respond to that last comment, but she knew what she had to do to get answers from Don.

Chapter 65

Don took the sleeping Millie cradled in his arms to her bedroom. He pulled back the covers, placed her on her bed, and removed her shoes and socks. Emilia barely became aware of her familiar surroundings, took one look at her daddy towering over her, smiled, and snuggled up with her teddy bear. She was sound asleep in seconds.

Don closed Millie's door behind him and began seeking out Valencia. He could tell she had been in the master bedroom recently. The clothes she wore that day were on the floor and her cell phone was on the bed. As Don entered the room, he could hear the shower running in the master bathroom. Don slipped into the bathroom stealthily and barely pulled back the shower curtain to get a view of his naked wife. She was washing her long, dark hair. Her eyes were shut and sheets of water ran over her face. Don followed the stream over her big breasts and down into the seams of her inner thighs. Valencia finally rubbed her eyes and started at the sight of a smirking Don.

"You ass! You scare me!" Valencia said.

"Why do I have to be all that? You're the one that started without me," Don fired back.

"Whatever. If you want to be here, you no go anywhere," Valencia said.

"I took Millie to the park. You knew where I was," Don said.

"You always play daddy."

"That's my job."

"You play one too many daddy. Who is Darius to you?"

"Who?" Don played dumb to see what Valencia knew.

"That girl! She say you name her baby Darius."

"She told you that?"

"No. She tell to Rich on Facebook. I see Rich page."

Don realized that there was something going on that involved public conversations about Mya's child-to-be. All unbeknownst to Don. Rich, who was supposed to be Don's friend, knew better than to publicly discuss anything about Don with other women. Don was just hoping that Mya hadn't disclosed that she was spending the summer in Florida. At least not publicly.

"Look, Valencia. I talked to her briefly the other day and gave her a few suggestions for baby names. From what you are telling me, she chose a name out of a list of names," Don explained.

"Really? Why did you talk to her?" Valencia asked.

"I consider her a friend."

"How you talk to her? You tell me she no have your number."

Don noticed that as the conversation went on, Valencia lathered herself at a faster, more aggressive pace. She was totally pissed.

"I still had her number. I'm sorry," Don said.

"You eh-stupid. Go away!" Valencia yelled.

"Why are you mad? This proves nothing."

"Don-Don, you no name a baby you think is yours. You name a baby you know is yours."

Chapter 66

Monday, June 22, 2009

Don didn't like the fact that he was close to having to decide between Mya and Valencia. To him, it was making a choice between his kids. Mya didn't see it that way, because she was willing to accept Emilia as her own child. But for Valencia, it was all or nothing.

Don looked at life differently than the two women he was involved with. Mya and Valencia both counted baby Ethan as among the living. To Don, if things could go wrong, they will go wrong. Case and point, Diana. And even if Ethan made it out okay, there was still a chance he could suddenly pass away. Case and point, Dejahmi. Basically, Don was virtually unwilling to risk what he had for something that wasn't guaranteed to pan out. He hoped that one day that Mya would understand.

Valencia and Don didn't celebrate their two-year anniversary that day. They avoided each other in icy silence; a passive-aggressive means of trying to punish the other person. Don didn't care. It worked in Mya's favor. It gave him time to think things through. Unfortunately for Valencia, he started to hate her all over again. Valencia, however, was determined to push the issue that day.

Valencia stood in front of the television to get Don's attention. Don was sitting on the couch with Millie sleeping soundly in his lap. Don stared through Valencia. He gave her a warning glare.

"If you want to talk, let's talk. But if you wake Millie, I will not be kind," Don said in a low monotone voice.

Valencia knew he was serious. His lack of voice inflections scared her more than his words. Valencia called it scary calm. She had rather hear him yell at her. However, that day, she was determined to be brave. She was going to be heard. Besides, she had the upper hand...right?

"I want deal. Make me deal," Valencia said.

"I'm listening," Don said.

Valencia pulled a piece of paper from behind her back.

"Here."

Don took the paper from her and looked over the handwritten document with the word "Contract" at the top. Don scanned it briefly and handed it back after seeing a few key phrases he didn't like: *"give up rights"*, *"Emilia and me"*, *"never see her again"*.

"What did you hope to accomplish here?" Don asked.

"You sign!" Valencia yelled.

Don looked over at Millie. Millie didn't move. He looked back at Valencia.

"Sorry," Valencia said softly. "Can we take her to bed?"

"Tell me what you want," Don said.

"I want you no see that girl baby."

"You asking me to be a bad father?"

"No."

"You think I'm a bad daddy?"

"No. I just no want that — it near my Millie."

Don stared silently at Valencia.

She flinched as if she saw a flame ignite in his eyes.

"So, I'm supposed to abandon this child?" Don asked.

"No...no se," Valencia said.

"You know I wasn't raised by my father."

"I know, Don-Don."

"Why would you ask me to do that?"

"Porque. She no family. Me and Millie family. I hate her."

"What did the child do?"

"Nothing. Baby innocent."

Don rubbed his hand over his head.

"Let me get this straight. You want me to agree to not raise this child. You get what you want. And I get nothing but the feeling that I'm a bad daddy," Don clarified.

"You get me and Millie," Valencia said.

"I already have Millie."

Valencia stood silently.

"Go. Take you little contract and find something that I can have," Don said.

"Then you sign?" Valencia asked.

"No promises."

Valencia left.

Don hugged his baby girl snug and released his hold. Don thought he saw her grin in response as she slept. Don smiled and kissed her on the cheek. He leaned back and noticed a droplet on his cheek. He wiped it away. There was another on Millie's arm. He realized something.

He was crying.

Chapter 67

Thursday, July 9, 2009

Don was eating a late-night meal after a long day at work. He was no longer on the truck crew. Within a few months, he was moved to the sales floor. His charisma made him approachable, which in turn made him likable. Don considered it a blessing and a curse at the same time. It guaranteed him a job. Nevertheless, it also netted him more responsibility with the same meager wages. His money paid all the bills. Valencia used her money to do whatever she wanted. Don never asked.

Don could see Valencia approaching him from his right. He ignored her and continued to eat his meal on the couch as he caught up on the latest sports talk on ESPN. Valencia stood there with a sheet of paper in her hand and waited for Don to acknowledge her. He eventually did during a commercial break.

"What you got?" Don asked.

"I fix it," Valencia said.

Don didn't attempt to take the paper from her.

"What does it say?" Don asked.

"I give you baby for her baby," Valencia said.

Don couldn't believe what he was hearing. He started chuckling to himself.

The audacity! Don thought. *She really thinks that's how it works.*

Don decided to test her willingness to go through with it. He stood up and approached Valencia. She looked up to read his face. She wanted to run because she was unsure if he was upset enough to do something bad, but his smile wasn't sinister. So, she stayed.

Don got really close to Valencia. He kissed her on the lips. She looked down and away. It wasn't the same. Her anger made Don a stranger to her. Don pulled off the t-shirt she was wearing, but she did nothing to assist him. She folded her arms across her exposed breasts. Don removed her panties and threw them behind the couch where the t-shirt was. Don then took a seat and went back to eating.

"We have deal, no?" Valencia asked.

"You tell me," Don said.

"You sign!"

"Get some clothes on. Come back when you have something you can actually do."

"You sign, Don-Don. Or I take Millie."

"Funny."

"If you bring that baby near Millie, I *kill* it!"

Don stopped eating immediately and stood up. He got uncomfortably close to Valencia once again.

"If you even think about that again…"

He didn't finish. He didn't have to. His eyes said it all.

Valencia started trembling. He kissed Valencia on her forehead and gave a facetious smile.

"Goodnight…wife."

Tr3.6.6

Chapter 68

Friday, August 21, 2009

Mya had returned to Texas for a few weeks. She wanted to look for a
place of her own, tie up a few loose ends with her job before she started,
and touch base with her family. Her family accepted the excuse she gave
them for spending so much time in Florida — she was hanging out with
Lisa and vacationing before starting her career. Foreman, on the other
hand, wasn't buying it. He just didn't have time to investigate the truth.
He had a hunch that it had something to do with Don, but, even if it
proved to be true, he could do nothing about it unless Don was in Texas.

———

Mya returned to Florida on a mission. She was determined to see
Don; and not just when he was ready to go to work. Well…she'd take
that too. But, she was craving sex with her boyfriend and refused to be
denied; she needed at least a moment of pleasure.

Don didn't work that day because he had to work that weekend.
Don and Valencia treated themselves to drinks at a nearby restaurant.

Don had to finish Valencia's margarita so that she could drive. The timer in Don's head was constantly ticking down. It wouldn't be long before his indecisiveness would blow up in his face. He hadn't had an alcoholic beverage in a long time. Well, long for him anyway. The combination of drinks made him numb. Which was fine because he was trying to drown out the many alarms ringing in his head that night — his temporary solution to a potentially huge problem.

He received a text from Mya shortly after he got to his apartment.

"I want to see you."

"When?" Don texted back.

"Tonight." Mya texted.

"Come get me." Don texted in reply.

"Already on my way."

Valencia ignored her inhibitions and wanted to take advantage of Don's lowered defenses. He hadn't signed the contract yet, but maybe with a little incentive, he'd be persuaded into making Valencia his priority. Her words. Then once he's proven himself worthy, maybe they would have a baby. Maybe.

Valencia hurried Emilia into bed so Don wouldn't spend hours watching Millie sleep and sobering up as he did it. She then undressed completely and put on her robe in case Don was going to shower.

She stood at the door of the bedroom. Don was sitting on the couch watching television, but, from where she stood, all she could see of Don was the back of his head.

"Don-Don?" Valencia called out.

"Huh?" Don replied.

"You sleeping?" Valencia asked.

"No. Almost," Don said.

"Come to bed, baby."

213

Don was about to get up when his phone vibrated. It was a text from Mya.

"Outside."

Don looked up at Valencia. He found himself in the middle of another bind. He had to make a decision.

"Not right now. I'm going for a short walk. Need to clear my head," Don said.

"Okay, baby. I wait for you," Valencia said.

Don had Mya meet him in the parking lot behind his building. When he got to the car, Don got into the passenger's side. She lunged at him and passionately kissed him. She could taste the alcohol on his breath. She didn't care. This was her chance.

She attempted to lay back and pull Don on top of her. She realized she was in the front seat.

"Get out," Mya commanded as she got out of the car.

By the time Don got out and closed the door, Mya was settling in the backseat and closing the door. She lay in the backseat and waited for Don. Don opened the door on his side to join her. Mya was propped up on her right elbow and reaching for Don's hand with her left hand. Don thought it was an awkward position. He tried sitting in the backseat and closing the door without touching her. Mya noticed his reclusive manner.

"You're not going to hurt me. Come," Mya said.

Don put his left knee on the seat and leaned forward between her legs to kiss Mya. He surveyed the size of Mya's swollen belly. He stopped short of kissing Mya when he felt his stomach touch Mya's. He flinched. Mya tried to take advantage of the new position he was in. She took off her shorts and panties simultaneously. She then quickly located his dick using only her hands as she studied his face for signs. Signs that he still loved her. She guided his dick inside her and lifted her hips to encourage him to give her deeper strokes and assist his irregular delivery. She couldn't tell if his face was weighted with concern, disgust, or if he regretted ever meeting her. Mya needed to know which.

"It's okay, babe. You're not going to hurt me," Mya said.

"It's not that. I don't have any room to do what I want," Don said.

Mya laughed pretty hard. It was more of a relief than a response to something funny.

He still loves me, Mya thought.

Valencia was sitting up in bed when Don returned from his encounter with Mya.

"You okay, baby?" Valencia asked.

"Yeah, I'm fine," Don said.

"Come here," Valencia said.

Don crawled into bed next to Valencia. She opened her robe, leaned over him, and brushed her breasts across his face as she often did to wake him. Don smiled.

"That's better," Valencia said. "I love when my honey smile."

She kissed and sucked on his neck in an attempt to arouse him.

Nothing.

She then pulled his shorts and boxers off and put Don's dick in her mouth. It took a tremendous amount of restraint on his part to keep Don from laughing as she made 'mmm' noises as if she liked what she was tasting. Don wasn't sure if Mya would want him to stop her or not. It's not like he asked Valencia to do it. Instead, Don just lay back and let his thoughts take him elsewhere until he drifted off.

Chapter 69

Friday, October 9, 2009

Mya woke up early to prepare for her hospital stay at Parkland. She was already six days past her due date. She didn't allow the nurses to induce her the week before; she was trying to give Don a chance to make it back in town. He still hadn't made it. She texted Don that morning to get him talking to her and eventually determine where he was.

Mya talked her mother into preparing a big breakfast. Mya wanted to gorge before she checked herself in. Working at the hospital was enough to turn her off the food there. After breakfast, Mya took one last tour of her room and the garage to make sure everything she needed was in the car. By the time she stepped foot in her childhood home again, she would have welcomed the newest member of the family into the world.

Mr. Brown insisted on driving Mya to the hospital. Mya was somewhat annoyed when his driving turned the eleven-minute drive into what seemed to be nearly thirty (according to Mya). She could almost swear that he caught every red light on purpose. Fortunately, she would not remain in his care once she reached Parkland.

Cathy had nurses waiting with a wheelchair for Mya at the door when she arrived just before eight. Mya was thankful that she didn't have to walk. She was still full from breakfast. Cathy handed down a stern warning: if anything went wrong during Mya's stay, heads would roll until she couldn't fire anyone else. She was still feeling the effects of losing Diana and her grandchild. Cathy didn't have any other children, so Mya was as close as she was going to get via Don.

When Mya was wheeled to her room, she found an array of flowers and cards from staff, former classmates, and friends. She knew that none of the flowers were from Don. Don knew better. However, she was disappointed that he hadn't sent a card. Unless he was hiding in the bathroom. Or maybe he was coming in after she got settled. He would be there. Her words.

Mya exchanged her clothes for two gowns. Two. One to cover her front and the other she wore backwards to cover her backside because no one needed to see her backside. Her words. She was thankful that Cathy gave her a double room with an extra hospital bed. That way Don could sleep next to her and baby Ethan. She would get rid of her parents somehow and he'd show up some time after that. She hadn't determined if he was in town yet. She sent him a text saying, 'Hey.' She wanted to give him an update.

Brenda walked in the door.

"Hey, General Nosey!" Brenda said.

Mya laughed.

"How long have you been waiting to say that to me?" Mya asked.

Mya's phone vibrated.

"I've been holding that one for a while. You happy to see me?" Brenda asked.

"What? No," Mya said looking at her phone.

"*Excuse me?*" Brenda said.

Mya looked up. "What? Oh, not you. Yes, I'm happy to see you, Brenda. *You-know-who* texted me, asking if we have a baby yet."

"Oh. Tell that boy to get his skinny behind up her and find out. We'll sneak him up here through the E-R entrance," Brenda said.

"Will do. What's on the agenda?" Mya asked.

"Girl, are you ready to have this baby or what?"

"I'm ready, but I don't feel...ready down there."

Mya's phone vibrated.

"You ready to have your water broken?" Brenda asked.

"No way!" Mya said.

"Mya Brown—"

"Oh! No, no, no. I'm talking about what Don said. He said he'll climb through the window so he'll go undetected."

"Girl, tell that boy to hush and get on up here. But, you? You need to tell me when you're ready."

"For what?"

"To break your water and get this baby out!"

"Oh, right. Yes. I'm ready."

"Mm hm. Make sure your head is out of the clouds by the time I get back."

Chapter 70

Brenda took charge of everything. She even told Mr. Brown when it was okay to be in the room and when it was not. Mya's mom, Virginia, was welcome to stay except when Mya needed to talk to Brenda about Don.

Mya hadn't dilated much at all from her expected due date. So, a few hours after Brenda broke Mya's water, she had Mya walk around the hospital for an hour. Senator Brown was proud to escort Mya, along with Virginia. It was the first time that she felt like he was actually playing dad in public instead of campaigning. That was a comforting thought. What was disturbing was having Brenda know her on a more than personal level now. But, Mya knew she was being well cared for. Seven hours into her stay, Brenda checked on Mya's progress.

Nothing.

"Girl, I'm so mad at you," Brenda teased.

"I'm sorry," Mya said with a chuckle.

"I know what you're doing and you need to stop," Brenda said.

"What are you talking about?" Mya asked skeptically.

Brenda leaned in close. "You're trying to hold on to this baby until Adonis gets here."

Mya laughed; however, Brenda's words made her think. On some level, she felt that subconsciously she could be doing that. Mya didn't want to admit to something like that to Brenda though.

"I hope you don't believe that. Is that your medical analysis?" Mya asked.

"You sure?" Brenda asked.

"I'm sure."

Brenda turned and headed for the door. "Girl, if you want my help with this baby, you better let go of him before seven because I'm going home."

"Thanks, Brenda!" Mya called out after her. Mya was grateful for everything that Brenda did to keep Mya comfortable. She allowed Mya's family to smuggle in a Philly cheesesteak sandwich for Mya's lunch. She kept all students away from Mya's room; including resident doctors. This was not the time for them to gawk or practice. This is real life. Brenda's words. Mya's only complaint, and it was minor, was that Brenda put the IV in Mya's hand instead of her arm. Pet peeve.

Out of curiosity, she asked Don via text if he could be there before seven. He replied that he wished he could but he couldn't. Mya took it as that he could possibly show up. Just not before seven.

Brenda had also started Mya on a Pitocin drip to induce more contractions and to help her reach full dilation. Even after being on it for hours, Mya hadn't progressed enough to give birth. Her contractions, however, were nearly on top of one another, which caused her great pain. Mya was set on not having an epidural as a part of her birth plan. She discussed it with Cathy ahead of time. Mya did agree to a lesser narcotic that could be given intravenously. Mya was less than satisfied with the effects of the drug. After a short while, she asked for another dose. Another nurse informed her that she could only have one more dosage, but she had to wait an hour. Mya asked for Brenda, but the nurse informed Mya that she was Brenda's replacement for the night. Mya looked at the time on her phone. It was only 6:13.

So much for seven, Mya thought.

Brenda's replacement, a slender white woman in her mid-forties named Stacy, suggested that Mya reconsider getting an epidural. Stacy and Brenda had discussed it shortly before Brenda left for the evening. Brenda believed that Mya would be a lot more comfortable if she got one. Mya rejected the idea at first. She feared the risk of complications more than she feared the pain of not having one. Stacy reasoned with her, stating that Cathy and Brenda would never allow it if they thought Mya would be harmed in any way. Stacy also spouted a few statistics that Mya already knew — the rarity of complications. It did little good. However, when the second dose of painkiller failed to help her, Mya changed her mind. Even after agreeing to it though, she had to wait another hour for the anesthesiologist to show up. Emergency C-section.

Great, Mya thought. *This is not how I pictured it at all.*

Chapter 71

Saturday, October 10, 2009

When Mya opened her eyes, she could see Don sitting in the chair next to her. He must have noticed her eyelids move because he walked over to the bed to get closer and hold her hand. Don didn't say a word initially. He just lovingly stared at her. Mya was too weak to move. She felt numb. She couldn't even turn her head to see if she was still pregnant. So, she tried to speak to Don. Don kissed her hand.

"Mya," he said.

Mya couldn't speak. She couldn't move. She could feel Don rubbing her hand, but she couldn't respond.

"I'm so proud of you, Mya. I'm here. Let's deliver this baby. You're doing so good," Don said.

She could finally turn her head. She saw her toes, but her swollen belly was missing. She turned to Don to ask what he meant, but she couldn't speak.

"I'm right here. Let's bring this baby out," Don said. His mouth was moving, but the voice didn't belong to him.

Mya closed her eyes, squeezed them tight, and then opened them up again. There was Stacy rubbing her hand.

"There you go," Stacy said.

Mya had apparently been dreaming. She looked towards her feet, but her swollen belly obstructed her view. She was still pregnant for the moment. One detail of her dream that did prove true was the fact that she was numb from the stomach down. The anesthesiologist feared Cathy so much that before the first dose of epidural could take full effect, he administered another one. He didn't want Mya to give Cathy an unfavorable report about him. Unfortunately, Mya would have a tough time pushing from places that she couldn't feel. And according to Stacy, that time had arrived.

Delivery took about twenty minutes. It wouldn't have taken that long if Mya could feel her legs and if her contractions weren't weak and irregular. The stress of it though caused the baby's heart rate to drop substantially. Once he was out, the doctor worked on trying to get baby Ethan to breathe. Mya noticed that she couldn't hear him crying. Virginia Brown did too and naturally gravitated to the table where the doctor had him.

Mya watched her mother's worried face and prayed that they would be hearing cries soon. She didn't know why, but she thought that Don's presence would have made a difference. Then again, it was best that Don wasn't there to witness that moment given his traumatic past. After what seemed like several minutes, baby Ethan announced his arrival with a cry. He made it. He was going to be okay. The only thing that would have made that moment better was Don being there.

Where are you? Mya thought.

Tr3.6.6

Chapter 72

Because the feeling hadn't returned to her legs, she couldn't participate
in giving baby Ethan his first bath. Her arms still worked, so she did
breastfeed him — a process that proved more painful than she imagined.
She spent most of the morning floating between the conscious and
unconscious worlds. It was unclear to Mya who actually visited her and
who she dreamed was there. Don hadn't answered her texts in a few
hours. She wanted to believe that meant he was on a plane or trying to
surprise her.

Mya was resting when Stacy came in to ask if she was feeling well
enough to have a visitor. Virginia Brown was in the room with Mya.
When Mya asked who it was, Stacy informed her that the man asked not
to be identified, said that he was a good friend, and that his arrival was a
surprise. Mya looked at her mother. It was a silent request that she leave.
Virginia knew that look. Virginia assumed that look meant that the
visitor was Don.

"Oh, why can't I be here when he comes? I like him," Virginia
said.

"I know, Mom. But, he won't stay long if you're here. He knows you're married to Dad the Senator," Mya said.

"But, I don't want to miss seeing father and son together," Virginia said.

"I'll record it. I'll take pictures," Mya said.

"Who's going to take a picture of all three of you?"

"He will. We'll manage, Mom."

"Can I at least hide in the bathroom? I won't say a word."

"What good will that do?"

"Call my phone and put yours on speaker so I can hear you two talk about the baby."

"*Fine. Go!*"

Virginia scurried off into the bathroom. Mya apologized for the circus act and asked Stacy to show her guest in.

Mya called her mom's phone, which wasn't on silent, but Virginia managed to answer it before anyone came in. Mya thought about fixing her hair, but she didn't know what it looked like to begin with. It didn't matter. Don was going to say that she was the most beautiful woman that ever gave birth, anyway. At least he better. It took nine months, a lot of puke, and three stitches to have his baby. She deserved the compliments. Her words.

Mya thought about making light of the fact she had really bad contractions at one point. She was going to tell him the story about Stacy bringing in a rocking chair and how it didn't offer any relief, so Mya rocked harder and harder until she almost flipped the chair. Then there was the exercise ball she sat on and nearly fell off countless times. He would surely laugh at that. Maybe. She liked it when they laughed together. But, he didn't have to laugh. Mya just wanted to be together.

The door opened. Foreman walked in. Mya was disgusted at the sight of him.

"I'm expecting someone, so now is not a good time," Mya said.

"Oh really? The nurse didn't tell you?" Foreman asked.

"Did he leave?" Mya asked.

"No," Foreman said.

"What did you say to him?"

"I know not who you speak of."

"Where is Don?"

"Now, why would he be back in town? He doesn't think I'd let him waltz right in here without taking him down, does he?"

"Where is he?"

"Why do you think he's here?"

"The nurse said I had a visitor—"

"That refused to give his name," Foreman finished while approaching the bed.

"It was you?" Mya asked.

"Yeah. That's funny because the nurse told me that you think I'm the father of your baby."

"In your dreams!"

"Is that so farfetched? You have been generous to me when you needed me to cover for you."

"You're sick."

"Oh come on, Mya. I watched you grow up. I watched you bathe. Watched you sleep."

"Get out."

"Let me have a little peek under the gown." He leaned over Mya.

"Get out!"

"Nothing that I haven't seen before." He reached for her gown.

"Leave, Foreman," Virginia said from the doorway of the bathroom.

"Yes ma'am. Just coming to check on Mya. That's all," Foreman said. "I figured you were with the sen—"

"Save it. I heard the entire thing," Virginia said as she approached Foreman.

"Come on, Virginia. I was giving Mya a hard time," Foreman said.

"You can blackmail me. Fondle me. Grope me. Even fuck me. But when you lay a finger on my baby, nothing you can tell my husband is worth that," Virginia said. "Get out."

"If that's the way you want to play it," Foreman said.

"Out!" Virginia yelled.

Foreman left without saying another word.

Virginia hugged Mya tightly. Tears streamed down both of their faces. Virginia grabbed Mya by the face and looked directly into her eyes.

"Does Adonis know about this?" Virginia asked.

"No. Well…he doesn't know the whole story," Mya said.

"I'll take care of it. Not a word, you understand?"

Chapter 73

Sunday, October 11, 2009

While Mya and Ethan were checking out of the hospital, Adonis was in Florida trying to keep his mind off what was going on in Texas. That was proving to be difficult. Mya had sent him a picture of baby Ethan swaddled in a hospital blanket the day he was born. He kept staring at the picture on his HTC One cell phone. Don sent it to his mother and a few friends. He was secretly a proud father. He even showed Emilia the picture of baby Ethan and explained that he is her little brother. Millie focused on the possessive clause of the phrase and deemed Ethan "My Eatin". She tried. Nevertheless, she was a proud big sister.

Don was too embarrassed to tell Mya his reasons for not showing up at the hospital. Financially, because he was paying for everything in Florida, he couldn't afford it. Valencia would never agree to give him money to go see Mya, let alone the baby coming out of Mya. Additionally, there was the risk he could have been locked up just for being in Texas. Then, there was the trauma issue.

Losing another child scared him more than anything. Truth be told, Don stressed over Millie until she turned two years old. He wouldn't let people touch her, babysit her, give her food, play with her, nothing. That is except for family members (which included Cathy) and even that took a while. Don acted as if sudden infant death syndrome was contagious. Don feared that more than Mya feared needles and insects. It was just something he couldn't get past and no one could tell him anything that would make it better.

Don didn't work that day. He spent most of his day doing whatever Millie wanted to do. Millie liked to play a game where she would pretend to serve her daddy imaginary beverages without revealing what the drinks were until he took a sip. Don had taught Millie that he had an allergy to milk. So, if Millie revealed that the drink was milk, Don would pretend to be sick until she ran to the imaginary refrigerator and served him some juice — the apparent antidote. Millie got a kick out of it and would giggle hysterically, while she kept her daddy guessing when she would say milk.

Don didn't intentionally ignore Mya's phone calls the day before. He had to go to work, cover for a co-worker, and could not get to his phone. He still felt bad. He felt like a deadbeat for not being there. Both of his kids were equally important to him. He just wished that he could get Valencia on board the happy family train.

Chapter 74

October 12, 2009 — July 22, 2010

Don let the next nine months go by without stepping a foot on Texas soil. Valencia seemingly rewarded Don for not attempting to go back. They did more things together as a family. Orlando Studios. Disney World. Even little things like dinner at restaurants. Movies. Bowling. Things they never used to do. Valencia spent lots of money trying to spoil Don. She bought him a huge plasma TV for his birthday. A PS3, multiple games, and accessories. A new laptop. Lots of clothes and shoes. Don never asked Valencia for it, but it seemed to make her happy to do it so he let her.

Mya tried including Don on every date she deemed important between the two of them. She texted Don on his birthday as if Ethan was the one who sent the message by addressing Don as Daddy. She included a recent picture of Ethan. Don made sure to acknowledge Mya on her birthday via text as well. Mya texted Don on their second anniversary. Don belonged to her no matter where he was. She felt that in a perfect world, with no complications (namely Valencia), Don would be with Mya and they would raise their two kids together.

During those nine months, Valencia hadn't attempted suicide or self-mutilation. It was the first time since Don had known her that had proved to be the case. Don didn't want to make a big deal of it by celebrating. Instead, he gave Valencia more than the usual attention. He wasn't sure if she just forgot or if she was waiting until she could get away from Don. Either way, Don considered it a victory once a month had passed.

Cathy was disappointed that Don was unable to meet her at Diana's memorial on March 26th. She knew where he was. She just wished that things were different. She missed Don. She was thrilled to at least have Don's junior around (as they called Ethan because he favored Don so much). Don, on the other hand, was starting to move past Diana for the first time. It was hard enough balancing two women. Not to mention the kids that came with them.

Valencia made a big deal about throwing Millie a birthday party in April. Don had already bought Millie a bike before her actual birthday. Don's philosophy was a person shouldn't have to wait to get gifts twice a year. So, birthday or not, Don couldn't really care less. Valencia invited kids and their parents from the daycare Millie attended. They did the whole singing and cake deal, but Don wouldn't allow Valencia to light candles on the cake because of the superstitious connotations that are rooted in Spiritism. He didn't like that.

Don and Valencia spent their anniversary at home watching movies on Netflix. Don let Valencia pick out the movies but commented that the ones she chose were borderline porn. She insisted on watching the movies in bed so they could emulate what they saw. Don poked fun at the unrealistic scenes and ruined the fun in it. Valencia didn't mind too much.

Valencia bought Don an onyx wedding band to replace the white gold band he had. Don wasn't expecting it. He thought it meant that Valencia was hoping to start over.

July of 2010 made ten months since Don had signed Valencia's contract, agreeing not to see Ethan. In what amounted to an exchange, Valencia was supposed to have another child with Don. Despite all the sex they were having, Valencia still wasn't pregnant. Don didn't investigate as to why. Although he signed Valencia's document, he never intended on adhering to it; he didn't expect Valencia to hold up her end of the deal either. If Valencia happened to get pregnant, he would have three children, but for the time being, he was a proud father of two. He just didn't show it very well.

Valencia, though, was satisfied with having her man. She felt like she won. That is until Mya came back to town.

Chapter 75

Friday, July 23, 2010

Mya wasn't alone. Ethan was with her. And Virginia Brown. And Mya's older sister, Ashley. They were all there for one reason — to make sure Don had a chance to see Ethan. Now, individually, they each had their own opinion of Don, how well they thought it would go, and if the meeting would actually take place. Ashley doubted Don would show up at all.

The Brown women had a room at the Holiday Inn Express on West Colonial Drive. Mya gave Don a heads-up about her mom and sister being there. However, Don wasn't intimidated. His mother just so happened to be in town that week. Don wanted to take Millie, but he didn't want to alert Valencia. He initially told Valencia he was going to check on his mother and that she was having a few issues. Taking Millie would only complicate things.

Don arrived at the hotel first. His mother wasn't too far behind, so he waited for her before he went inside and up to the second floor. Don texted Mya as he approached the door. He expected Mya to open it without him having to knock. She didn't. Don knocked hesitantly as he rechecked the room number on his phone. Ashley Brown opened the door. He had only met Ashley once before. She acted as if she wasn't impressed by him at all and somewhat annoyed. Mya emerged from the back room as Don and his mother entered. She was busy changing a diaper so she missed the text.

Payback?

Introductions went all the way around. Don didn't say much. Donna Lane did all the talking. She and Virginia traded baby stories about Don and Mya to determine whom Ethan took after. Donna was a human DNA tester. Her words. She could determine the paternity of a baby just by looking at the alleged father and the child. She studied Ethan as he played with toys on the floor. Don and Donna were on the floor with him.

Ashley noted how Don seemed to show no interest in Ethan. Donna was the one trying to get Ethan to come to her by picking up one of the toys he had before him. Don did nothing but return a toy that had ended up out of Ethan's reach. What Ashley didn't realize was that Don was building trust with Ethan.

Don knew Ethan could see him. At one point, Ethan touched him accidentally when reaching for a toy in Don's hands. Don didn't immediately try to pick him up, which made Don approachable. Don didn't set parameters for Ethan; such as making him play near Don so that Don could play with Ethan. Donna, however, did all of that. Thus, when Donna picked Ethan up for the first time, he whined.

It took about half an hour before Ethan showed he was willing to share a toy with Don. Don obliged Ethan. He would push the toy to Ethan. Ethan would attempt to push it back. Don didn't talk to Ethan.

Don's only words came in response to questions Donna would ask about Millie. Donna was bragging about Emilia to Virginia.

Ethan then took interest in Don's apparel. His company ball cap. His arrowhead necklace. His lanyard with keys that hung from his neck. Don drew attention to those items by touching them one at a time. Don reached out and gently touched Ethan's arm. Ethan retreated, but turned around and noticed that Don didn't follow him. Ethan slowly came back. Don touched him again. This time Ethan retreated to where his mother was seated on the floor. Don acted as if he was ignoring Ethan and played with the toy Ethan left behind.

Mya encouraged Ethan to go back. Ethan was set on getting his toy back. He went back. Don let go of the toy and played with the keys on his lanyard. Ethan watched. Don stood as if he was going to leave, then leaned over and picked up Ethan.

The whole room grew quiet as the women watched Don and Ethan interact. Don took off his hat to avoid butting Ethan with the brim. Ethan took it as an invitation to put the brim in his mouth.

Cell phones came out all over the room. All of the women took pictures of the two males having a bonding moment. The women murmured amongst themselves. Don ignored them and enjoyed the moment with his son. Ethan dropped the hat to grab at Don's arrowhead.

"You like that?" Don asked.

Ethan looked up at Don. Mya got close for a picture and Ethan immediately lunged for her neck. She grabbed him and supported him on her hip. Don took off his necklace and put it around his son's neck.

Don then picked up his hat and headed out of the door with his mother. Mya walked Don to the elevator with Ethan in her arms. Don and Mya were out of the others' view. Mya's smile faded, which signified that she was going to kiss Don. Unfortunately for Mya, Don read her. Mya rocked onto her toes to be taller just as Don swung his head away to kiss his son on the cheek. Mya's lips followed Don's like heat-seeking missiles. They could both feel the heavy tension between them.

There was no ATM in the hotel so Don just gave Mya the cash he had in his wallet. He felt he had to. Don got out of there without kissing Mya. His mother was waiting for him in the parking lot.

"Boy...*he* is your son," Donna said.

"I know, Ma," Don said.

"I don't know what you're going to do, but you better take care of my grandbaby," Donna admonished.

"I will," Don assured her.

Just then, Don noticed that Virginia and Ashley were exiting the hotel. Don suddenly felt the urge to sneak inside and try to at least get a quickie in before Mya went back home. Don saw his mother off, but he realized that Virginia and Ashley were stalling. Don thought that they were on to his scheme. Virginia Brown motioned for Don to meet her at the passenger's side of the vehicle they were sitting in. Don walked over to the Lexus SUV. Virginia handed Don a manila envelope. Before Don opened it, Virginia had to tell Don something. What she told him made his blood boil.

Ashley drove the vehicle away as they left Don there to stew in his own rage. Don opened the envelope to find a black and white, 8x10 photo of a man that Don had only seen twice before. The next time would be the last.

Chapter 76

January 15-16, 2011

Things started to unravel between Don and Valencia for good just a week after Don met Ethan. Don was starting to get more attached to his phone, which took attention away from Valencia. Don was talking to Mya more often trying to learn more about Ethan. Don also arranged to put Ethan on his health insurance. Valencia sensed that Don's sudden distance and new expenses had something to do with Mya, so she began to investigate.

Don kept a lock on his phone and never left it unattended unless he was sleeping. Nevertheless, he did make a mistake. Don hadn't talked to his father in years. Now that he was having children of his own, Don thought he'd prepare a package with a quite a few pictures of Emilia and all the pictures he had of Ethan; including the ones of Don and Ethan that Mya took on her cell phone. He also enclosed a letter that detailed the kids' ages and birthdays. Although it was sealed, Don made the mistake of not mailing it out immediately. He put it on the bookshelf near the front door so he wouldn't forget to mail it out the next morning. However, Valencia waited until Don was asleep, opened the package, read the letter, and viewed all of the pictures. She started an argument with Don about it the next day.

By December, Don and Valencia were back to sleeping in separate beds. Valencia started new affairs with two coworkers. Don didn't care. He was content with avoiding Valencia and using that time to think more clearly. He was determined to end it with Valencia for good this time. He regretted not following through with his decision years before. His so-called fears amounted to childish excuses.

Don purchased divorce papers the first week of January. He was so proud of them that he took a picture and sent it to a coworker named Shawn. Shawn congratulated Don for finally going through with it. Shawn knew enough to know that Don's marriage was toxic. Don waited until he and Millie were headed to Texas before he broke the news to Valencia. Mya assured him that it was safe for Don to come home. Senator Brown no longer trusted Foreman and wouldn't back him in his quest to have Don put away for any amount of time.

On January 15th, Don handed Valencia the divorce papers and the black onyx ring. Don told Valencia that he and Millie were leaving and didn't plan to come back. To his surprise, Valencia actually cried. What Don didn't know was why Valencia cried. For Don? For Millie? Or for both of them? Don didn't tell Valencia where they were going, but she assumed it was Dallas. Don advised her to catch a cab to retrieve her car from the airport. He didn't allow Valencia to see them off.

Don and Millie arrived at the Brown's Highland Park home on Emerson Street at 11:45 at night. Mr. Brown opened the front door as Don approached it with Millie in his arms. Mya watched from a short distance behind her father. Mr. Brown led them to a spare bedroom and went back to his own room. Mya waved as she disappeared behind her bedroom door. Don made a mental note of where each room was.

Once he was inside the bedroom with the door shut, Don breathed a sigh of relief.

"Daddy, I want to play SpongeBob on your phone," Emilia said.

She had slept most of the trip there so she was wide-awake for the moment. Don gave Millie his phone. She knew how to get the app she wanted on her own. While Millie strummed away on his phone, Don took off her jacket and shoes and placed her on the pillow next to his.

An hour later, Don was still awake staring at the ceiling as if he was looking for a sign. Millie had been sleep for nearly forty minutes. That's when he heard a noise that sounded as if something had slid across the floor. He sat up and walked towards the door. There he found a manila envelope. Inside was a note with an address and a brief message:

It happens tonight.

Chapter 77

Don sat up suddenly as if he had awakened in an open casket. He calmed down at the sight of Millie. She was still sleeping.

Must have been a bad dream, Don thought.

It was only 7:38 in the morning, but the rest of the house was teeming with alert people. Don then became aware of a soreness in his neck and a massive headache. Millie sat up when she noticed Don wasn't next to her anymore. Don picked her up to carry her to the bathroom. The extra weight added to his own exposed a back injury. He felt as if he was jumped by a mob of gangsters.

After helping Millie wash her face and brush her teeth, Don led her into the living room where Virginia watched Ethan crawl around and push a toy truck. Millie immediately got on the floor and joined him. Ethan studied Millie for a moment with a curious grin. Although she was bigger than he was, Ethan recognized she was a little person like him. Millie talked to him kindly and called him by name. He didn't know who Millie was, but he was intrigued by her.

Don smiled as he watched the two interact. That was easily the best moment of Don's life up to that point. Virginia was touched too. She didn't want to ruin the moment, but she took advantage of the opportunity to talk to Don alone.

"How did it go?" Virginia asked quietly.

"Business as usual," Don said.

"There's aspirin in the medicine cabinet. Any major issues?" Virginia inquired.

"Nothing I can't handle. I'll take some aspirin, though," Don said.

"She's so beautiful. Isn't she beautiful, honey?" Virginia said. She was alerting Don of Mr. Brown's arrival. He and Mya had returned from the store.

"Yes, she is. I see that they are getting along quite nicely," Mr. Brown said.

"Of course. I wouldn't have it any other way," Don said.

"Hi, Millie," Mya chimed in.

"Hi," Millie said without taking her eyes off the toy cash register she discovered.

Mya got on the floor with her. "What do you have there?"

"This is uh…money for the food and juice and candy," Millie explained.

"Can I buy some milk too?" Mya asked.

"Yeah, but Daddy lergic so he can't have none. Daddy drink juice," Millie said.

Millie's explanation brought laughter to all the adults in the room. Millie proved to be wise beyond her years, which spoke well of Don and lent hope to the youngest member of the family.

"Well I hope your daddy isn't allergic to eggs because I made some for breakfast. Are you hungry, Millie?" Virginia said.

"Yeah," Millie answered.

"Good. Go wash your hands with Daddy and we'll get you something to eat," Virginia said.

Don didn't eat until later that afternoon when the Browns ordered pizza. Don wasn't comfortable there. Mr. and Mrs. Brown afforded Don and Mya time alone with the children in the den.

Even with two screaming kids running around, the sexual tension between Don and Mya was intense. At one point, they found themselves alone in the kitchen. Mya did her zeroing-in number, but Don let the moment pass by turning his head to avoid the kiss. Besides, their view was impeded by the refrigerator. They could have easily been caught kissing if they got lost in the moment. However, while they were sitting close and sharing a blanket on the couch, Don convinced Mya to slip underneath the blanket and give attention to his dick with her mouth. The kids were still chasing each other around the house and Mya's parents were in the living room, just around the corner.

That afternoon, Don and Millie entered the spare room they were lodging in. He closed the door, reached into his jacket, and pulled out a small jewelry box. He opened it to gaze at an engagement ring featuring a two carat, princess cut diamond on a white gold band. Millie took a glance at it and went back to poking around on Don's phone.

"What do you think?" Don asked her.

"We should call, Mom-mom," Millie said.

"Okay," Don said and then put away the ring.

Don dialed the number and allowed Millie to talk for a while. Millie didn't reveal where they were nor did she mention Ethan by name. She just talked about playing and what she ate. Millie then signed off and handed the phone to Don.

"Hello," Don answered.

"Hey. Where are you?" Valencia asked somberly.

Don heard (what he assumed to be) a voice in the background.

"Who's over there?" Don asked.

"No one," Valencia said.

"I heard someone talking."

"What? No one here, Don-Don."

"I'm on my way back."

"When you get here?"

"I don't know. I'm not close."

"Please bring Millie home."

"Yeah, whatever."

Don hung up the phone. His ego got the better of him. He was convinced that he heard a man's voice in the background. In the apartment he paid for. He had to get back and set her straight. His words.

Don and Millie walked in the living room as Mya and Virginia discussed dinner plans. They were planning as if Don and Millie would be there. Don announced otherwise. He claimed that Millie's mother was having an episode and that they needed to get back. He also cited a forecast of heavy snow as the reason for their immediate departure. Virginia could tell he was lying, but she thought it had to do with something else he was hiding.

Mya followed Don and Millie to the airport. Don left Mya some money for Ethan. She had rather he stay than leave money behind. She tried convincing him to stay at least one more night. She was hoping to try to get him to meet her somewhere so they could extinguish the sexual tension. However, Don was set on going back to Florida for reasons that didn't make sense to Mya.

Before they checked in for their flight, Don clutched the jewelry box inside his pocket. He looked at Mya for a sign. Nothing. He didn't know what to do. Maybe it wasn't time.

There's still time...right? Don thought.

Don kissed Mya as if he would never see her again, and then turned to leave. He called himself stupid all the way home. He knew Mya loved him and all she was asking for was one more night. Why should he care if Valencia had someone at their apartment? He had done the same thing with Mya.

Don checked his phone once he hailed a taxi outside of Orlando International. He had a missed call from Mya. She left him a message on his voicemail. Assuming that Mya was confessing her love for him over the phone, Don checked the message immediately:

"Oh my goodness, Don! I don't know if you heard, but two people we know died from alcohol related car wrecks last night. Rich was one of them. I'm so sorry, babe. I know he was your friend. The other guy used to work for my father. Jason Foreman. I'm not heartbroken about that at all. But, isn't that crazy? Anyway, call me when you get this. I love you."

Chapter 78

Sunday, February 13, 2011

Donna Lane's hospitalization brought Don back to Dallas. Don, Valencia, and Emilia flew in on Friday the eleventh and lodged at Donna's home instead of checking into a hotel. Don insisted that Valencia come with him given that it was so close to the thirteenth. He wasn't convinced that she wouldn't have another episode while he was gone. She complied without disputing and expressed her concern for Don's mother. Don was hoping to see Mya while he was in town. He found out that she was in Nebraska visiting family. Apparently, she had a lot of family members there. Don commented that he didn't know black people lived in Nebraska. But, then again, Mya was mixed.

That Sunday morning, Don tried to make sure that Valencia stayed in good spirits. He made plans for them to take Emilia bowling at one that afternoon. He had flowers, candy, and a small teddy bear delivered to the door and made sure Valencia was the one who answered the door. She was taken by surprise. She secretly hoped the gifts were from someone else. She felt somewhat guilty that Don extended his kindness to her despite the fact he was trying to divorce her. However, it wasn't enough to keep her from going forward with her plans to meet up with Jarin. She told Don that she wanted to go to the mall to return some jeans. She didn't return until ten that night.

Valencia was relaxing on the couch after being out all day. Millie had slept most of the day away so she had plenty of energy when her mother finally came home. That morning, Don had told her that they were going bowling when her mother came home. The lanes closed at five. Valencia had taken the only car they had to meet up with Jarin, so Don didn't get to take Millie bowling; let alone check on his mother.

Millie didn't understand and was throwing a temper tantrum because her mother had failed her. Don didn't correct Millie. He allowed Millie to let her mother know how selfish Valencia was in so many words. Don was getting ready to take a trip to the hospital. Millie was driving Valencia crazy by running around the couch in endless circles.

"Chase me!" Millie called out to her mother as she tagged Valencia on the leg. Millie took off running again.

Valencia ignored her and continued texting on the phone.

"Chase me, Eatin!" Millie called out to Valencia as she tagged her on the leg again.

Valencia caught the name, paused, and glared at the little girl touching her leg. She then kicked Millie in her chest. The force was enough to cause Millie to leave her feet. Fortunately, Emilia landed on a throw pillow that was on the floor behind her.

Don witnessed the whole thing. Before he could think of anything to say to Valencia, he was at Millie's side, checking to see if she was okay. He picked up his daughter delicately and cradled her in his arms. Millie was shocked, but she didn't get a chance to cry. Daddy already had her safe in his arms. Don carried Millie to the bedroom on the first floor. Valencia offered an apologetic look, but Don didn't see it. His focus was on Millie.

Don called Brenda at home to see what he needed to do to make sure Emilia was okay. Brenda instructed Don to gently apply pressure to each of Millie's ribs to see if Millie was experiencing any pain. Emilia reported no such thing nor did she flinch. Brenda explained that it could take up to two weeks before any internal injuries would show up on x-ray. Brenda then expressed her disgust for Valencia and told Don to keep a closer eye on Emilia from that point going forward.

After Don hung up with Brenda, Don sat on the bed next to Emilia and talked to her for a while. He tried to talk about other things that had nothing to do with Valencia kicking her. But, just before Millie went to sleep, she brought up the subject on her own.

"Daddy?" Millie said.

"Yes, baby?" Don answered.

"Mom-mom be bad to me," Millie said.

"I know, baby. Daddy sorry," Don said.

"Daddy…can you spank Mom-mom for me?" Millie asked as she drifted off to sleep.

Don felt his eyes stinging. Tears streamed down his face. It hurt him to think of his baby girl feeling wronged as she did. How did she know what spanking was? And why did she think that spanking was the answer for something that was done maliciously? Don never spanked her. Valencia never even thought of spanking Millie while Don was around.

Don started thinking back to a time when he was at home alone with Millie and she accidently knocked over a cup of milk. Millie froze with a worried look on her face. Don just smiled, but he noticed that her face expressed worry and dread. Don assured her it was okay, and asked her how they would fix it. Millie ran to the kitchen, brought back a towel, and together they cleaned up the mess. Don then hugged her and told her it was all better. But, then Millie asked if she still needed to go get her mother's belt. Don made sure she understood that it was not necessary and treated her to ice cream for cleaning up the mess like a big girl.

The thought of Valencia abusing Emilia disturbed him. He kissed the sleeping girl on the cheek, tucked her into bed, and turned off the light. He then stopped by the kitchen before heading for the upstairs bedroom. As he walked by the couch, he asked Valencia to help him with something upstairs. He didn't explain what. She only heard his voice since the lights were off. She sent one last text and went upstairs to meet Don with her phone in hand.

When she entered into Don's dark bedroom, she was struck on both sides of the head with two quick punches. The first was enough to make her fall, but the second one stunned her to the point where she thought she saw a light flash. She hit the floor without being able to break her fall with her hands, and, as a result, her head slammed on the ground. Don then delicately tied her hands behind her back with a necktie. He used another to tie around her head to serve as a gag, and a third to tie her ankles together. None of them were tight. Don then turned on the light. He had a kitchen knife in his hand.

Valencia was scared half to death. However, unlike the last time she claimed Don had beat her, this was real.

Chapter 79

Wednesday, January 16, 2008 — 2:54 AM

Don had slept for a little over an hour. Rich helped Valencia get Don onto the bed. She quickly dismissed Rich and undressed Don while he was unconscious. She stripped him down to his boxers, went through his pockets, and sniffed his clothes. His phone had a lock on it so that proved to be fruitless. She then pulled out his dick and smelled it to see if she could tell if he had been having sex. Nothing. She let it go for the moment and crawled into bed wearing only a t-shirt.

She reminisced about how she used to wake him up by giving him head as he slept or by riding him until he woke up and realized it wasn't a wet dream. She missed doing that. She thought for a moment that maybe Don missed it too. So, she got on top of Don and put his dick in her pussy. She rode him for a while, but it wasn't the same. Back when the relationship was young, she knew he loved her. Or did he? Whatever the case, they were happy then.

She lay beside him, stroked his head, and waited for him to show signs of waking up. She gently traced his facial features with the tip of her fingers. He used to like when she touched him like that.

About an hour after she crawled into bed with him, Don woke up. He was still very drunk. He had to pee. Valencia followed him to the bathroom. He tried supporting himself on the wall behind the toilet, but he was leaning too severely. He was trying to aim his stiff dick towards the toilet. Valencia stood under his left arm so Don could brace himself. Then she used her left hand to aim the stream into the toilet.

He didn't even notice. He was still glazed over. Valencia still tried communicating with him. She wanted him to touch her and show he loved her while his guard was down; while he was under the influence. Alcohol was his truth serum and Valencia knew it. She propped his body on the doorjamb and used her weight to keep him upright.

"Don-Don…Don-Don, look at me…look at me," Valencia said.

"What?" Don grunted.

"Don-Don, do you love me?" Valencia asked.

"Fuck you," Don said.

"Why, Don-Don? Why fuck me?"

"You know why."

"What make it better? I say sorry, you no like. I say everything."

Don didn't respond. His eyes were closed.

"I do anything! Please! Wake up, Don-Don! I do anything! I be your slave," Valencia said.

"I hate you!" Don said.

"No hate! Please, Don-Don. You…you can beat me. I do what you say. Here, I be your sex slave."

Valencia turned around and lifted her shirt. She held onto the doorjamb with one hand and grabbed onto Don's dick with the other. She then shoved his dick into her ass and pushed off the doorjamb to make it go further. Don sensed the feeling and opened his eyes. He locked his knees and let her do all the work.

"What are you doing?" Don asked.

"Shh...just fuck me," Valencia said.

She watched Don over her left shoulder. He really wasn't into it. She tried going faster to see if that would excite him. It made him dizzy.

"Get off me," Don said.

"Not yet," Valencia said.

"Get off!" Don yelled.

"No," Valencia said.

Don put his hands on Valencia's waist to stop her from moving, and lifted her off his dick. When he pushed her forward, she hit the right side of her face on the doorjamb and fell to the floor. Don went to the sink to vomit. Valencia got up and hit Don on the back and shoulders.

"Just fuck me and I'll leave you alone!" Valencia screamed.

"Don't...touch me," Don said calmly.

She backed away.

"I'm sorry, Don-Don. Here, let me help you," Valencia said as she helped him to the bed. He fell asleep pretty quickly.

Valencia went to the mirror to look at her face. There were no marks, but her face was sore. That's when the idea came to her.

She went back to the bed and watched Don sleep. She picked up his arm and dropped it to make sure he was sleeping soundly. He didn't move. She remembered a movie she watched with Don where a crazed lover beat herself with fruit in a sock. Valencia repeatedly hit herself on the right side of the face with the back of Don's hand. Afterward, she finished what she started by shoving Don's dick into her ass once more and rode him until he came inside her.

Tr3.6.6

Don didn't know any of that. His memory of that night came and went in hazy glimpses. When he finally came to his senses later on that day, all he had to go on was Valencia's story and her swollen face.

Chapter 80

Sunday, February 13, 2011

Don sat down on the floor in front of a bound Valencia and talked to her in a calm voice.

"You know you really fucked up this time, huh?" Don asked.

Valencia tried to talk, but Don held up the knife and hushed her.

"Don't wake up my baby. I have three rules. The tie in your mouth means no loud talking, no screaming, or any of that. You stay calm and I'll remove it. The tie around your hands is rule number two. Don't hit me and I won't hit you. And finally, there's rule number three. No kicking unless you want me to do to you what you did to Millie. Understood?" Don explained.

Valencia nodded her head to indicate she understood.

"Good. By the way..."

Don knocked Valencia on her back. He took the knife and used it to cut off her shirt and her bra.

"How do you feel? Exposed? Embarrassed? That's how I feel being married to a whore," Don said.

Suddenly, Don cut off a lock of Valencia's hair.

"That there was for Millie," Don said.

Don then threw the knife across the room and covered his face. He looked up to make sure Valencia was okay, untied her hands, and told her to untie herself. He stepped away from her and sat down at the desk he used to do his homework at. Valencia noticed that the ties around her mouth and ankles were tied like shoestrings. Even in anger, Don showed mercy. Valencia crawled over to Don, hugged him around the waist, and sobbed with her head in his lap. Don was not sympathetic.

"Get off of me," Don said calmly.

"No, Don-Don. Please. I'm sorry," Valencia said.

"Now you're sorry? Ha! Funny," Don said sarcastically.

"I do anything! I show you," Valencia said and tugged at his shorts and boxers.

"Please don't make me get you off of me."

Valencia ignored him and started sucking his dick.

"Get off of me," Don said calmly.

Valencia stopped only for a moment to ask, "You no want?"

"You wanna know what I want? I want a divorce! Just let me go! Please, just sign the papers!"

Chapter 81

Tuesday, February 15, 2011

Don woke up coughing violently. He was in a tub full of crimson water and had eventually slid down to the point where his mouth was level with the water. With the exception of shoes and socks, he was fully clothed, but the water was now cold. He shivered as if he woke up in a frozen lake. He felt a sharp pain as he attempted to lift himself by bracing his arm on the side of the bathtub. Don located the source of his bleeding — a deep cut just half an inch from his ulnar artery. This was no accident. The memories leading up to the gash started to flood his mind.

—

The next morning after Don chastised Valencia for kicking Emilia, the family went about life as normal. They went to visit Donna Lane at Medical City Dallas Hospital on Forest Lane. They were there for less than an hour before it got awkward. Valencia was unusually quiet and reclusive. Valencia ignored Millie when Millie called out to her. She acted as if Millie was a sibling that got her in trouble with their parents. Donna commented on Valencia's behavior, but Don didn't care to explain. Instead, he complied with Valencia's wishes and dropped her off at Parkland to visit former coworkers. Don didn't notice that she left her phone in the car until he was back at Medical City.

Don returned to Parkland with Millie to pick up Valencia around four that afternoon. She was nowhere to be found. That alarmed Don, but he didn't panic. She knew people in Dallas. Don figured she hooked back up with Lisa who was back in town at that point.

Later that evening, Don heard a knock on the front door of his mother's house, shortly after he put Millie to bed. Don was in the upstairs bedroom. When he looked towards the window, he saw the familiar flashing lights of police cars. He didn't go to the window or answer the door. They left. Don decided to call the police to inquire why they were there. They informed him that Valencia was at the station reporting a domestic dispute and that they were there to conduct a wellness check on Emilia. Don told the police that he was out town and that Millie was safe inside the house. He also lied and said that a neighbor was checking in on her.

Knowing that the police were on their way, Don sprang into action in an attempt to get away. He wasn't going to leave Millie stranded, but he had to allow the police to see that she was okay and remain hidden until they left. So, Don kissed his daughter on the cheek and climbed into the attic through the access in his closet. He took his phone and a spare blanket up there with him. From the closet, he could watch for anyone entering his room and he could see Millie.

The police used Valencia's spare key to get inside the house. Donna Lane made sure Valencia had one when she and Don got married. The police searched the house for Don. Nothing. One officer picked up Emilia and carried her out to Valencia. Other officers collected evidence of the reported assault — knives, neckties, the shirt, and the bra. Don stopped watching to make sure they couldn't find him. He fell asleep while he waited for them to leave.

Don woke up around 11:30 that night. He searched through the house and discovered that the police took all of Valencia's belongings out of the house. Emilia's things were missing too; likely at Valencia's request. Don wasn't sure exactly what Valencia had told the police, but he was sure that, if she went to this level of betrayal, she must have said something serious.

Don was upset that he hadn't done more to make sure Millie didn't end up in the enemy's hands. He was supposed to protect Emilia by any means, but he didn't. In his mind, he deserved to die.

At midnight, Don tweeted a cryptic message:

Today I become immortal.

The message scared the hell out of Mya who tried desperately to get in touch with Don. He wasn't answering. Don went to the bathroom carrying a small kitchen knife. He filled the tub with slightly hot water and got in. Don didn't know how quickly he would die; he just knew that he would. So, Don thought of the last songs he wanted to hear before he died.

He didn't want to hear anything upbeat. He was a fan of Boyz II Men's "On the Road Again" so he played that. Then "Don't Let Me Fall" by B.O.B. Last, he played "Fucking Perfect" by Pink. He recalled that a woman cut herself with a razorblade while sitting in a bathtub in Pink's music video. While the song was still playing, he pressed the knife to his arm, counted to three and sliced. The shock of the pain made him drop the knife in the water. He bled profusely. He couldn't see how deep the wound was because of the amount of blood but he hoped it was enough. He lay back and waited to die. About four songs had played and Don didn't even feel woozy. He found the knife again. He placed the knife in the wound and pressed down harder this time. He counted to three.

One. Two. Three...

He didn't move. He had to get over the pain mentally and go through with it. He had to die.

One. Two. Three...

Still no movement. He couldn't get out of his own head. He could see Mya, just across from him, begging him not to do it, and promising things would work out. But to him, those were merely optimistic lies. Millie was gone. He had failed. And failure was not an option.

Do it now! One! Two! Three!

Slice.

The loss of blood caused him to pass out, but it wasn't enough to kill him. Now, Don was on a mission. But, in order to complete his mission, he had to see if Valencia was dumb enough to go back to their Florida home.

Chapter 82

Tuesday, February 15 — Monday, February 21, 2011

Don wanted to try to remain under the radar as much as possible. Therefore, he decided to take a bus via Greyhound to Orlando. Don had to wear a light jacket so that his sleeves would cover the bandage he used to wrap around his wound. The police had no idea that the wound existed, but had they returned to Donna Lane's home looking for Don, they would find a bathtub full of bloody water. Don neglected to drain it. He was in a hurry to get out of town.

The bus station in downtown Dallas was just like any other across the nation — filled with low-income people. Don found it funny that these same people had no vehicles, yet were shelling out hundreds for their smart phones and data plans. Don tried to keep a low profile; however, the lowered brim and grey, hooded jacket drew more attention than he expected.

Two women headed to Louisiana approached him and invited him to stay a couple of weeks with them in New Orleans. Mardi Gras was approaching. Some of the residents there were looking to get an early start. Don entertained the two women with conversation. He declined the invitation, stating that he had business to take care of in Florida. If he could have, he would have boasted of how he was going to prevent Valencia from taking another breath ever again. He was dead set on it.

Travel time was 27 hours, which meant that Don would probably be very tired by the time he got there. Fortunately for him, there were hotels within two miles of his apartment; just in case the police were staking out at his apartment.

Don arrived in Orlando shortly after seven Wednesday evening. Don called his trusted coworker, Shawn, for a ride from the bus station to his apartment complex.

Don surveyed the scene before approaching his apartment. Valencia's car was not in the parking lot. There weren't any strange cars with people inside them in the middle of the night either. When Don reached the door of his apartment, he pressed his ear to it to see if he could hear any movement on the other side of it. Nothing. Don attempted to use his key to unlock the door. The lock didn't turn. The locks had been changed.

Don got a sudden surge of adrenaline. Paranoia set in. He wasn't sure if he was being watched or not. He felt as if the police were steps ahead of him, just waiting for him to show up. Valencia wasn't smart enough to do this on her own. His words.

Don checked into the Holiday Inn Express for the night. He didn't want to stay in one place for too long. Don opted for a late checkout so he could grab lunch at Wingstop. After lunch, he arranged to spend the night at Shawn's house. Don snuck out at night and broke into the apartment on West Colonial. No one noticed. He discovered that the apartment was vacant for the most part. All that remained was four trash bags of Don's clothes and other belongings. Don called a taxi and hauled his bags of items to Shawn's house.

The next day, Don tried staking out Valencia's workplace. Even after hours of being there, she was nowhere to be found. Don didn't know how he was going to get back. He borrowed Shawn's truck knowing that he didn't know how to drive a stick. Don barely made it there after watching a short tutorial on YouTube. He didn't intend on going back though. Don figured that he'd catch Valencia coming or going, kill her, and turn himself over to the local authorities. But, since she wasn't at work, he'd have to locate her.

Don tried calling Valencia. Her number was changed. It looked as if Valencia was winning every round of the battle. Don knew that all it meant was she was good at running. She was still naïve. Don called her workplace the next afternoon pretending to be the electric company, calling for a current contact number. She gave him her new phone number.

Gotcha! Don thought.

Valencia caught on shortly after she hung up with who she believed to be a representative from the electric company. It was something he said, or maybe it was the way he said it, that caused Valencia to recognize Don at the last second. Nevertheless, she was sure it was him.

Dallas Police alerted the Orlando Police that Don might be in the area. Don was now a person of interest in the break-in and a suspect for crimes committed in Texas. Orlando Police were tracking Don's movements through his cell phone service.

On Monday morning, they correctly guessed that Don would try to get Emilia back. They tracked him down right outside of Millie's preschool on West Oak Ridge Road. Don was on the sidewalk. Multiple cars converged on him, blocking his paths. He was trapped. Because there were kids in the vicinity, Don knew that the police wouldn't shoot him. Or would they?

Don reached for a bulging object in the right pocket of his jacket. Two officers shouted commands to show his hands. Don didn't comply. Another officer ushered children, parents, and teachers inside the building. Other officers blocked off traffic to prevent other parents from approaching the premises. The standoff continued. The officers shouted commands once more. Don remained defiant.

You deserve to die. Make them shoot you.

Finally, a woman nearby who shook loose from the officers got Don's attention.

"I don't know you. But, please. Please just do as they say. Please," the woman said.

Don was just about to draw on the officers. But, there was something about the woman that reminded him of Mya. Mya. The woman he suddenly forgot in a blind rage, while being hell-bent on revenge. Don put his hands up and surrendered. The police quickly moved in and handcuffed him. Once he was under their control, one officer checked his pockets for the weapon he was threatening to use.

A cell phone charger.

Chapter 83

Thursday, December 24, 2015

It had been nearly five years since she had been able to touch him. And although a lot had happened since then, Mya could never forget the day that she laid eyes on Don for the first time.

Mya and Don lost contact in 2012. Lack of communication. Don didn't expect her to wait for him, yet Don felt that if she loved him like she said she did in her letters, then she wouldn't form any type of relationships with other guys. She did. Don took that as a clear indication that she didn't care. Regardless, he was serving a five-to-nine-year sentence in Avon Park, Florida for an array of crimes in Texas and for breaking and entering in Florida. The State of Texas allowed Don to serve all his time in Florida despite him being convicted of more serious crimes in Texas.

As Don slipped into an emotional abyss, it seemed his life, as he knew it, took a turn for the worst. All of his grandparents died within a year of each other. His cousin was murdered. A DNA test proved that

Emilia was not his biological child. And if that wasn't enough to crush his soul, his mother, Donna Lane, lost her battle with cancer and died.

Don was numb. He joined a fight club within the prison just to get a high off the adrenaline it took to obliterate a bigger opponent. After he came down, though, he would sink deeper within himself.

Don was like most inmates in that he used exercise to keep his mind off of what was going on beyond the confines of the institution. Yet, one day, out of nowhere, Don got the notion to call Mya. It was in July of 2015. Don was prepared to be cordial, yet direct. He was determined to stay on topic. Ethan. That was all he wanted to inquire about. Ethan was five at the time, which meant that he and Don could have an actual conversation without the baby talk. Don suspected that Ethan might be mild-tempered, smart, and well-spoken.

The phone calls were only twenty minutes so Don didn't have time to talk to him. He made arrangements with Mya to talk to him the next time. To Don's surprise, Mya asked many off-topic questions. She even inquired about his relationship status. Don of course made sure he threw in there that Mya was his last girlfriend since 2012. He hoped it stung a little, but it didn't seem to affect her. Mya also revealed that she was single.

Over the next few months, the phone calls became more frequent. Don used some of his prize money from fighting to acquire a smuggled cell phone just so he could talk to Mya and Ethan.

Late at night, Mya and Don openly spoke about their former relationship and their sexual encounters. At times, the conversation got so intense that they would both seek relief via masturbation. At other times, the conversation touched on past issues between them and often left someone crying. Most of the time that was Mya.

Mya could tell Don wasn't the same. He was a more fragile version of Don that just happened to have forty pounds of extra muscles that he didn't have before. She definitely approved. He was still witty. Still an ass when he wanted to be. But emotionally, he was more forthcoming than he used to be. And he was more sensitive to the things that Mya said or did.

For instance, Don became suddenly ill when Mya revealed there had been guys after Don. Or when she brought up things about Ethan that Don didn't know, he'd be brought to tears. Don made it clear from the outset that Mya was all he wanted out of life. Mya wasn't too sure. Don had lived a double life for so long that it would be easy for him to do it again. Moreover, if Valencia was still in the picture and Millie was proven to be his child, Mya felt that she probably wouldn't be a priority like she wanted to be. Not that she necessarily wanted to be a priority to Don. But to somebody. Yet, Don would get his shot.

Don was to be released on Wednesday, December 23rd. And despite the holiday travel, he would have plenty of time to catch a plane and meet Mya at their designated spot — room nine-eighteen.

After some negotiating on both sides, Don and Mya decided to resume their relationship. Don was ready and willing to settle down and marry Mya immediately. Mya, on the other hand, wanted to use the meet at room nine eighteen as a test run. She was looking for something specific. She couldn't put a name on it, but she knew it when she felt it. It used to be, when he was near, her body would brace itself as if Don was going to taser her. Her stomach sank. Her palms started to sweat. Her pussy would throb. Her lips twitched. Her eyes nearly crossed as she focused on his mouth. The air between them became heavy and when he touched her, she could almost see sparks fly. Her words. Despite being with other men, she never felt that way with anyone else. She was hoping to revive that with Don.

After taking Ethan to her parents' house Thursday afternoon, Mya stopped by the Highland Park hotel on Mockingbird Lane to confirm her reservations. Then, Mya checked to make sure Don's flight was scheduled to arrive on time. On Tuesday, Don told Mya that he didn't need a ride from the airport to the hotel. Don was known for downplaying things as if they were not so bad. That worried Mya. She hoped that the 'little scuffle' he mentioned that left him with a 'small gash' didn't actually mean that he was in need of medical attention. She hadn't talked to him since then, but that was to be expected. He was leaving the phone behind since he was being released Wednesday morning. Don told Mya that he would be there no matter what, even if he had to walk. All Mya had to do was sit there and look pretty until he arrived. His words.

Mya checked into the hotel at 6:50; an hour before Don's plane was scheduled to arrive from Florida. However, Don still hadn't arrived at the hotel at 9:03. Mya was scantily clothed — an old t-shirt from Don and some lace boy shorts was all that covered her body. Her eyes were getting heavy so she slipped under the covers and waited for Don to arrive.

Chapter 84

Mya awoke to the sound of a knock on the door. She looked at the clock on the nightstand. 11:16. There was a knock again. Don would normally pick up his key from the desk, so Mya wondered if it could be someone else. Maybe they had news about Don. Hope and curiosity led her to the door. Pleasant surprise. It was Don.

Mya leapt into his arms. Don took a few steps inside and closed the door behind him. Mya kissed him hard. Don responded. He put her back on her feet and backed her to the near wall. He removed the shirt she was wearing. Her golden skin seemed to shine in the dim light just as he remembered. Her breasts were still full. Her nipples greeted the touch of his cold skin. Don kissed her lips then allowed his lips to make their way past her neck and to her breasts. He softly teased her nipples with his tongue. Mya grabbed his head with both hands and pulled him into her breasts until Don inhaled a mouthful. Don then grabbed both of her hands and pinned them against the wall.

Next, Don lowered himself onto his knees and slowly pulled off Mya's sexy panties. Don enjoyed the visual because they served as a see-through barrier that housed the goods. His words. Don lifted Mya's right leg and put it on his left shoulder. This allowed him to lick Mya's pussy at an angle. Don went at Mya's clit with his tongue. Mya enjoyed every bit of it. To give him a more direct shot, Mya put her left leg on his right shoulder and braced herself against the wall. Mya thought it felt too good to be true. She tried to pinch herself, but Don grabbed her hands and made Mya hold onto his head. He then supported Mya's back and stood on his feet.

Mya let out a squeal as she felt herself become airborne. This was new to her. It was new to Don also, but he shared this fantasy with her one night when they were talking on the phone. Mya remembered it. She also remembered that she was supposed to be angry with him because he was late, but she couldn't stay mad after all that he was doing to her. It was as if she had coached him on exactly how she liked to be pleasured. He hadn't missed from the second he placed his tongue on her pussy.

Truth was, however, she would be mad at him. That is until she found out that Don never made the flight home to Dallas. He never made it to the airport in Florida. He never made it out of the prison. He never saw the light of day on Wednesday. She wouldn't get the news until sometime after she woke up. But, for now, she was creating memories with the love of her life. Enjoying Don as she used to. The way she was meant to. In a way that no one could take away from her.

Sweet dreams, Mya Brown. Sweet dreams.